A PARTRIDGE IN SUNSHINE BAY

JEANINE LAUREN

Littleford House Books

A Partridge in Sunshine Bay

Copyright © 2024 by Jeanine Lauren

A Partridge in Sunshine Bay was first published in Canada and around the world by Jeanine Lauren. This is a work of fiction. Similarities to real people, places, or events are entirely coincidental.

ISBN: 978-1-0689038-3-0

Cover Design by 100 Covers

CHAPTER 1

*N*eville, a little white Westie, sat inside the door of Tom Jones's woodworking shed and whined.

"What's wrong, boy?" said Tom. "You miss Joe?"

Neville looked up at him, wagging his tail in acknowledgement. In his experience, humans liked it when he interacted. If he was good, maybe Tom would let him outside where he really wanted to be. He tried asking. *Woof.*

"Sorry, boy. Joe won't be back for a few days yet, but I'll take you out soon."

Out. Tom said *out.* Neville stood on all fours, wagging

his tail harder, and barked again, excited that they were speaking the same language.

"Wait, young fella. I've got to finish sanding and painting these decorations. They have to be ready for the Community Tree Festival on Saturday. Then we can take a break."

Neville stopped wagging his tail and sat down. *Wait*. He hated *wait*. That word meant he wasn't going out. He whined again. Sometimes whining made humans reconsider.

He looked up at Tom, but Tom was ignoring him, so he stopped and shuffled closer to the door, waiting as the sandpaper went back and forth. That noise was better than the scroll saw Tom had used earlier that day, but it was still irritating. He lay down by the door and held his paws over his ears. That was better.

But what was that scent?

He crawled closer and sniffed at a crack in the door. It was that cat! He jumped to his feet, ready for action.

That cat shouldn't have been here. It wasn't her territory. So he warned her off. *Yap! Yap! Yap!*

"Neville, shut it!" Tom exclaimed.

Neville looked up at him and wagged his tail, then barked again.

"Neville!"

Woof, Neville said half-heartedly, just to make a point. He turned around three times and lay down at the door again, still sniffing the air. The cat was still out there, so he growled a bit.

"Neville," Tom warned, and Neville stopped, put his head on his paws, and kept sniffing the air.

A few minutes later, steps crunched on the cold gravel that lined the drive to the workshop. Neville jumped to his feet again and wagged his tail. He knew those footsteps. They belonged to Clinton, Tom's son. Clint was staying with Tom while he worked on a new building at the college.

"Dad, you out here?" Clint pushed open the shed door.

"Clint! Don't let the dog out!"

But Clint wasn't quick enough to stop Neville from wriggling through his legs and dashing out into the yard. Neville barked and headed straight toward Angel, the black cat, to teach her that this was his territory, not hers. He was determined to make sure she left.

Angel froze a moment, turned toward Neville, then dashed back toward her house.

Neville took off, joyful in the chase, his fur streaming back from his face, and let out a quick bark. Finally, he had the cat in his sights. He had tried three times before to catch Angel, and he'd failed. This time, he was sure he had her.

He ran past Tom's house and into the yard that belonged to Vivian Woolf.

Vivian Woolf was someone Neville liked to avoid. She didn't like four-leggeds of any sort and was always growling at Joe whenever they went for a walk, even when Neville barked in his friendliest voice and wagged his tail.

"Keep that dog off my lawn," she said almost every day, and Neville had learned to do his business in the park down the road or, in an emergency, in Joe's yard near the back fence.

Today she was there again when Angel ran between her and the trash can she was pushing to the curb. Neville didn't slow down. He followed the cat between the rolling can and the woman's legs and breezed through the gap, but not before he heard her scream.

"You damn animals!" Then he heard a crash, but he didn't look back. He had to catch the cat before she got to the fence between her yard and Joe's. He knew from experience that once she got to the fence, the chase would be done, and he would have to wait until next time.

"Vivian, are you okay?" Tom's voice floated on the wind rushing against his face as he sped toward the fence. Only a few more steps and he would have the cat. But before he reached Angel, she leaped with those sturdy legs of hers to the top of the fence. She turned and looked back at him, scoffing in that way cats do when they best you, then hopped down out of sight, leaving him to stand in front of the fence, barking.

"There you are, you little devil," said Clint a moment later. And before he knew it, Clint had snapped the leash onto his collar and was forcing him back to Tom's house.

"Keep that dog away from me," yelled Vivian as Clint led him back to Tom's house. "He's a menace."

She was lying on the ground, and Tom was hovering over her with a puzzle-solving look on his face. He used that expression when he was in his workshop, trying to make something work.

Soon Neville was back in the house, locked in his sleeping cage. Clint returned outside, leaving Neville to pant and lay down with his head on his paws. Soon he was dozing from the exertion, dreaming of catching his prey and barking happily in his sleep.

CHAPTER 2

*E*ight o'clock on a Wednesday morning was not the ideal time for Claudia Woolf to receive bad news. Especially not today, when she had an important presentation to make about a project she had been working on for months.

But Alex Banting, her boyfriend of six years, had other plans.

"What did you say?" she asked, gripping the granite counter of the kitchen island they had installed the year before. She needed balance as her life quaked.

Alex furrowed his brow and set his briefcase on the floor beside him. He ran a hand through his newly cropped hair. "I have an interview today for a job in Victoria."

"Victoria?" She gasped. "I was just promoted six months ago. Here. In Vancouver. Where we live. I worked for years for this opportunity."

"I realize that," he said. "But this job…"

"Is in Victoria," she repeated.

"Is in family law," he said.

"You don't work in family law. You're a corporate tax attorney."

"And I haven't been happy for a long time. That's why I've been taking courses to prepare for a career change."

"You said you were taking courses to further specialize in contract law."

"What made you think that?" His brow furrowed further.

"You told me you were taking courses to specialize."

"Yes. In family law."

"So you're talking about a career change?" She must have heard him wrong. How could he have planned such a drastic change without her knowing about it?

"Yes, that's what I just said."

"Why didn't you tell me?"

"I told you I didn't like what I was doing. I told you I was exploring options. I told you I was taking courses. What exactly didn't I tell you?"

"The part about moving back to Vancouver Island. The part about looking for work away from here."

"Claudia, we talked about that, too. We talked about buying a house outside the city. A place to raise kids."

"But not right now."

"If not now, when? I'm forty-three. You're nearly thirty-eight. When did you think we'd start?"

She stared at him. Why, on today of all days, was he doing this? Well, if he wanted to start something, she was loath to disappoint him.

"I can't believe you. You know what I've been through this year. Why would you put this pressure on me now?"

He walked toward her and reached to pull her into an embrace. "That's not what I intended."

She put her hands up and stepped back. "Well, you could have fooled me."

His arms dropped to his side, and he looked at her, the clock on the wall in the kitchen, and then the door. "We should talk about this later."

But she was just getting started. "You know this year has been hell. With my dad dying, and me finally getting my promotion, I haven't had time to think about moving, or children, or any of those things."

"That's true. You haven't had time," he said calmly. "But while you've been busy, I have been exploring my options. This interview is an opportunity."

"What is that supposed to mean? Your options? Am I not to be included in this?" She felt her voice rise almost involuntarily. *Calm down.*

"You're twisting my words now," he said. "Of course I meant *our* options."

"I haven't been too busy to discuss things this important," she said, more loudly than she intended. Her control was breaking, and if she didn't walk away, she might end up yelling. He was considering moving away and leaving her no alternative but to choose between him and her career. Her heart was pounding hard now. How could she have missed this?

"Yes. We have been too busy," he said, his voice still steady. It made her want to scream in frustration. "Think about it. When was the last time we went out together without it having to do with work, or family, or friends?"

"It's been a busy year," she said, "with Dad dying and Adrian's heart attack."

"And your promotion, and my increased workload and courses," he added. "It's been a lot, and we've not had enough time to discuss what's important."

"Well, you should have made time," she spat. "Dropping this on me first thing in the morning is wrong, Alex."

"I know. I was intending to talk to you about this tonight. I shouldn't have said anything. I don't even know if I have a chance at the job. I haven't got a lot of experience in the field."

"I don't know what to say," she said, tears pricking at the corner of her eyes. "I guess we both have a lot to think about."

"We'll talk properly tonight," he said, reaching toward her.

"You'd better go." She stepped back and nodded toward the clock. "We'll both be late." Then she walked to the bathroom to get away from him and stared into the mirror until she heard the front door click shut. "You are not going to cry," she told herself in the mirror. She forced a smile that made her reflection look ghoulish, which only prompted bitter laughter while the tears started to fall.

She grabbed a tissue and dabbed at the tears before they ruined her mascara, then walked to the door, picked up her bag, and left, putting the pain of their conversation firmly in the back corner of her mind. She had a meeting to prepare for. There would be time enough to think about this later.

Ninety minutes later, Claudia stood at the threshold of the meeting room. She double-checked that she had everything and took a moment to breathe. The funding committee for the Brighter Horizons Foundation, where she had worked for the past twelve years, waited on the other side of that door. As their new director of new initiatives, she needed to make a good impression and gain approval for this latest project. The family and youth society she had been working with for six months was counting on the funding. Their plan for a teen transition project had all the elements required by the funding committee, but she had seen plans like this rejected before.

Still, she had to try. It would make a big difference to teenagers getting ready to leave school. The project would offer them career counseling, work experience, and training in a variety of trades. The society was even lining up apprenticeships so they would have work, guidance, and a cohort. It was a perfect plan all around. And if the committee approved the funding, she would oversee the contract as part of her new portfolio and witness the results firsthand. That was what made the job worthwhile.

All she had to do was convince the committee that this was the best project to run this quarter.

She was about to step into the room when her phone rang. It was Alex. She didn't want to talk to him. Their fight that morning had already overwhelmed her. He knew she was nervous about this pitch and yet had picked this morning to bring up the idea of moving, something they had vaguely discussed only once months ago. She didn't have the energy or time for it now, so she sent him to voicemail.

The phone rang again. Frustrated, she picked it up to shut it off when she noticed a new caller: her sister. Karen rarely called—and never on a weekday unless there was something wrong. Her thumb hovered over the button to send the call to voicemail, and then it rang again. What if Karen's husband Adrian had had a relapse? Though he had completely recovered from his open-heart surgery from the year before, something could have happened.

The phone rang a third time, and she sighed, accepted the call, and put the phone to her ear, stepping further down the hall so she could have some privacy.

"Hi," said Karen. "I need you to come home. Mom fell."

Claudia's heart hammered. Her sister was using that staccato speech she reserved for emergencies, and it always put her on edge. "What happened?"

"She was putting the garbage out on Monday and tripped over the neighbor's dog. Very inconvenient."

"Is she okay? Did she break a hip? Why didn't you tell me sooner?" Claudia asked, her voice tight with concern.

"She is just badly bruised and needs to rest. She didn't break a hip. And I didn't call you because she told me not to."

"So, if she obviously doesn't want me there, why *are* you calling me?" Claudia asked, the hurt of the past year resurfacing. "You're her favorite nurse and confidante." As soon as she said it, she felt bad. It wasn't all Karen's fault. Their mother was stubborn. But they had made an agreement that Karen would keep her and their brother Blaine updated as to their mother's welfare.

"I'm calling because I'm at the airport, about to board a plane to Mexico. Mom's friend Helen was supposed to look in on her, but she's stuck in Toronto in a snowstorm."

Claudia frowned. "What's in Mexico? Is there some kind of emergency with Adrian's uncle?"

"No, his uncle's fine. We're going on vacation."

"I don't understand." Sometimes her sister communicated so badly. "If you wanted me to come there, why didn't you give me a heads-up that I would be needed?

It's Wednesday. After what happened with Dad, I thought I could count on you to at least call if something happened to Mom."

There was silence on the end of the phone, and then Karen said, "I'm sorry. Mom said she didn't want to bother you. That it was minor."

"Dad went to the hospital with a minor ailment too, and look how that turned out."

There was a sharp intake of breath at the other end of the line. "I know you may never forgive me, but Dad didn't want us to see him like that. He was the one who kept it quiet for so long. He wanted one last good Christmas. He never even told Mom how sick he was. I refuse to be blamed for this anymore. If I'd thought Mom was in any danger, I would have called. She was just embarrassed at having tripped over a dog. That's all."

"What was your backup plan if I couldn't make it?" Claudia asked, peeved because, no matter how much she wanted to blame her sister, Karen was probably right. Their father had been just as stubborn as their mother was.

"I'd ask Tom Jones to look in on her, I guess. But I would rather it be you."

"Wouldn't it have been better to tell me earlier?"

"It's only for two weeks, and I didn't know that Helen was stuck in Toronto until half an hour ago. I don't know how long it will take for her to get home. Their flight was canceled, and it may be days before they can get another one."

"And Rhys? Is he going with you?"

"Rhys is still home. He has finals this month. He'll be fine. He's going to stay at Mom's at night."

Khalid, the executive director and Claudia's boss, opened the door to the conference room and stepped outside. "Coming?" He pointed at his watch.

"I have to go, Karen. Can I call you back after my meeting?" She could hear a loudspeaker in the background of the call.

"That's our flight," Karen said. "I just made you a reservation for the seven o'clock ferry. You don't have a choice, Claudia. Mom needs you."

"Why are you going now? It's almost Christmas."

"Adrian and I have a credit that expires at the end of the year. It's now or never." Her voice was muffled, but Claudia could hear Karen say, "I said I'm coming!" Then she could hear her more clearly again. "We'll be home on the twenty-second"

The twenty-second? Today was the fourth. "When does Jessie gets home?" Jessie, Karen's eldest, was in her first year of nursing at a university in Kelowna. "Surely she would be better help."

"Jessie doesn't get home until the twenty-third. I'm not sure how long it will be until Helen gets back." Then her voice was muffled again, her hand over the mic. "I just need to tell her about Rhys."

Khalid was striding toward her now, looking uncertain. The committee was waiting, and she had to go.

"What about Rhys? Can't he help until Helen gets there?"

Karen laughed. "Rhys is sixteen. He can barely look after himself. Mom was going to watch him, but now she's been hurt. No, I need you."

"Do you even care that I have a job? Things to do?"

"Claudia, you don't have a husband who needs a vacation after his heart surgery, and you don't have teenagers to worry about. It's not like anyone else is relying on you. That's why I didn't call Blaine. Besides, with the snow, I doubt he could get here anyway."

Claudia rolled her eyes at the mention of Blaine. Their brother lived out in New Brunswick with his wife and the three of his five children who still lived at home. He rarely came back to Sunshine Bay. The last time had been for their father's funeral ten months before. He wasn't likely to return soon.

"It's a busy week," she said. "I have some important meetings."

"Well, around my place, it's always a busy week. It's your turn." Another announcement came on in the background. "They're calling us to board. I'll talk to you in a few hours when we get to the resort."

"Can you at least email me contact information for Rhys, for the neighbors, and for Tom Jones, maybe?"

Karen laughed. "It's in your email with the reservation. And old Tom isn't Mom's favorite person right now. He's the reason she was in the hospital in the first place. Goodbye." And the phone went dead.

Khalid was now standing beside her, concern etching his face. "Everything okay?"

She quickly pocketed the phone and returned her focus to the task at hand. If she thought any more about the call, she would scream.

"Everything is fine. But I need to talk to you after the meeting."

CHAPTER 3

*K*aren hung up the phone and turned to Adrian. "I told you I was coming," she said.

"I know, but they're boarding."

"Since when did you become such a worrier?" she asked. Adrian never worried about anything. Probably because he knew she would look after the details. She always looked after the details.

"I really want to be on the beach, sitting in the sunshine right now. The only way that will happen is if we get on that plane." He grabbed her elbow and stepped toward the dwindling line for boarding, and she pulled her passport and boarding pass out of her purse.

"Are you sure we should do this? I wasn't counting on Helen not being back on time."

"Yes," said Adrian. "If we don't go now, we lose the credit for this trip, and we haven't been away in years."

"Claudia sounded stressed."

"Your sister will be fine," said Adrian. "And so will your mother, our son, the whole damned town." The woman at the counter was speaking into the loud-speaker. Last call for passengers. "Come on." He gave her a little push from behind, and she felt her anger rise. He really was pushy sometimes. Couldn't he see she was worried about her mother?

She handed her passport and boarding pass to the flight attendant at the gate and walked down the hallway to the plane. Adrian followed close behind with their shared carry-on bag. After putting their bag into the crowded overhead bin and settling into their seats, Adrian said, "Look, I know you're worried, but put a little faith in your sister. If she doesn't get there tonight, Tom will look in on your mother. He's been really anxious about her. I talked to him when I was over the other day with your mom's groceries."

"And Rhys?"

"He's the most grown-up sixteen-year-old I ever met. Remember, he's going to be on his own after he graduates next year. Stop treating him as though he's still ten."

"But what about food? What if Mom can't cook? I keep meaning to teach him, but he's always busy, I'm always busy. We just haven't been able to do it."

"I gave him some extra money this morning," said Adrian. "He can order pizza if he needs to."

"Pizza? You think fast food is the answer?"

"That depends on the question," he said, smiling. Then he patted her hand. "Stop worrying. I want you to enjoy this trip. Have fun. Dance, swim, read. Whatever you want to do."

"But what if something happens and Claudia can't get there?"

"Did you ever consider that it might just work out better than you expect? I wish you would just relax. After this plane takes off, you won't be able to do anything about it anyway."

"That's true." She looked up at the screen where the safety video had started, then double-checked her seat belt and glanced out the window. The plane was taxiing on the runway. If she wanted to get off now, she'd have to stage a medical emergency.

Adrian squeezed her knee, and she looked up at him. "We're going to have fun—two weeks of fun we already paid for. I want you to just sit back and relax."

She took a deep breath and did as he suggested. *Relax*, she told herself as the plane sped up. *Relax*. The plane was now in the air. *Relax*. She accepted the glass of wine Adrian ordered for her and chose a movie to watch, a comedy that she had seen before and loved. Soon, she was laughing.

She glanced over to see what Adrian was watching and found him looking at her with bemusement. "What?"

"It's been a long time since I heard you laugh like that," he said. "It makes me happy."

"Why don't you watch it with me?" she asked, handing him one earbud.

"Maybe for a while," he said, putting the earbud in his ear. They sat together, leaning on each other as they had for over twenty years, and enjoyed the show until he said he was going to take a nap for a bit.

"Okay," she said, grateful that he was paying attention to his limits more diligently than he had before his cardiac arrest. "I'll let you know when they bring us lunch."

He nodded and reclined his seat, still holding her hand.

And as he drifted off to sleep, she was grateful that he was still with her. If she lost him, she wasn't sure how she would move on. How was her mother even getting up in the morning? It had to be so hard. Maybe that was why her mother seemed to be slipping lately. And the fall hadn't helped.

Not for the first time in recent months, she wondered if she should push her mother harder to sell the house and move to supported living. She would talk to Claudia about it when she got back. Claudia would have a fresh perspective because she rarely came to visit. Then they could talk to Blaine and make a decision together. She was tired of trying to handle things all on her own. And, after failing to notify either of her siblings early enough for them to arrive in time to say goodbye to their dad, she couldn't afford to make the same mistake again.

Though she wasn't as close to either of them as she wished to be, they were still her family.

And she did care about them, no matter what they seemed to think.

CHAPTER 4

*V*ivian Woolf sat in the reclining chair she had purchased for her husband, Ned, two years earlier and stared out her picture window at the naked pear tree that stood in her front yard. She and Ned planted it when they had moved into this house twenty-five years before, and it had flourished. They had kept it pruned, and it had borne fruit—enough for her to preserve and enough to give away to friends and neighbors.

Today she felt like that tree must feel—naked, cold, alone. But where the tree was in hibernation, preparing to come back stronger in spring and bear fruit again in the summer, she felt as though all her resources had been stripped away. She leaned over to the couch beside the chair and pulled the quilt she had made for Ned the previous Christmas onto her knees. Still not warm enough, she pulled it up to her ears, wincing at the pain in her ribs, and felt the tears fall. She closed her eyes to block out the tree.

Her phone rang in her dreams. She squirmed until it stopped, and then she drifted further into oblivion. That was what she wanted. In the depths of sleep, nothing hurt, and sometimes, like today, Ned was there, sitting beside her, holding her in his arms.

Bang. Bang. Bang. The loud, insistent noise in the distance urged her to leave Ned, but she didn't want to go. So she thrust the noise away and settled again into his arms. They lay there together for minutes or hours until bells rang, and he loosened his grip. She came to consciousness, and the pain in her ribs made her catch her breath.

She opened her eyes in time to witness the last red glow of the sun slipping over the mountain in the distance. The phone rang again, and she felt around for it on the table beside her, finally answering it on the fourth ring.

"Mom?"

"Claudia?" she asked, her voice groggy.

"Are you okay? I've been calling and calling. Karen said you fell."

"I told her not to worry you about it." Why did Karen never listen? She should have minded her own business.

Claudia was quiet for a moment, but Vivian was sure she had heard the girl swear under her breath.

"Mom, I didn't know you fell until today. Karen called from the airport."

"Airport?" Why was Karen calling from an airport?

"Didn't she tell you she was going to Mexico?" Claudia's voice was tight with stress, so Vivian thought a moment.

"She said she was going a few weeks before Christmas."

"Yes. That's right. She's gone. It is a few weeks before Christmas."

Vivian was awake now. She peered at the calendar on the wall, with the aid of the light now streaming into the room from the streetlight outside. It still said November.

She could use her hospital stay to explain why she had forgotten to turn the page, but that would be a lie. She hadn't gone to hospital until the second of December. She hadn't turned the page because to admit it was December, the first December without Ned, was too painful.

"Mom? Did you hear me?"

She didn't answer, lost in memories of Decembers past. She and Ned celebrated every year, beginning on December first when they began putting up decorations, through to January sixth, when they would finally box up the festive wrapping and baubles. They had taken down the decorations together this year, carefully packing them away in the garage. Two days later, Ned had gone to hospital with the cancer he hadn't told her about, and by February he was gone, residing in the cemetery. Only seventy-five years old.

But not changing the month on the calendar hadn't kept December from arriving, and with it the reminder of her overwhelming loss. She closed her eyes, wishing for Ned's arms again.

"Mom, are you still there?"

"Yes. I'm still here." Her eyes fluttered open again. But she didn't want to be here without Ned. Life was naked and gray and dull without him. And now, as she tried to shift in the chair, she was in more pain than she had felt since she'd broken her leg at the swimming pool ten years earlier, after slipping on a flip-flop someone had left on the deck.

"Listen, I'm on the ferry," Claudia was saying. "I've arranged to work from Sunshine Bay. I'll be home around nine."

"What time is it?"

"Seven. The boat is just leaving. I'm coming. Rhys should be there soon. I told him to come and check in on you after his practice."

"Rhys is coming here?"

"Yes, as soon as he finishes band practice. They're getting ready for their winter concert next week."

"Okay," said Vivian. "See you soon." She hung up and closed her eyes again. Sleep. If she could just go to sleep, she would see Ned again.

"Grandma?" She woke to find Rhys shaking her arm,

looking down on her with wide eyes. The house was ablaze with light. Was it morning already?

"What?" she asked groggily.

"Oh, you scared me," he said, sitting down on the couch beside her. "When I came in, it was pitch black in here. Why didn't you turn on a light?"

"I fell asleep," she said, stating the obvious, then letting her eyes drift closed again. "I just want to sleep."

"Have you had dinner?"

She opened her eyes again and saw the concern on his face.

"No." she said. "Not hungry."

"Grandma, when was the last time you ate?"

She frowned, trying to focus on the question, then shook her head. "I don't know." She closed her eyes again. Why couldn't he just let her go back to sleep?

He got up then, and she heard him talking to someone in the kitchen. She didn't know what he was saying, but he was back too soon to bother her again. Now he was pinching her skin near her neck. She tried to swat him away.

"No, it doesn't spring back quickly," he told someone on the phone. "Okay, I will wait with her. Thanks."

"What are you waiting for?" she asked, her words slurring.

"The ambulance. They'll be here soon," he said. Then he got up and dialled his phone again. "Aunt Claudia? Yes, they're coming. I'll meet you at the hospital."

"Hospital? I don't want to go there. I just want to sleep." She tried to lever herself out of the chair before she remembered it was reclined. She fumbled for the button on the chair so she could lower her feet.

"Grandma," he said, looking at her closely, "I know you just want to go to sleep. Dad just wanted to go to sleep too. But you must wake up again. For me. Please." He was pleading, and she tried to understand what he was saying. "The ambulance will be here soon. Stay awake, Grandma."

"I just want to sleep."

"Have you had anything to drink? Water?"

"No," she slurred.

Rhys got up and went to the kitchen. Good. He was

gone. But before she could get comfortable again, he was back with some water. "Drink this, Grandma."

She grimaced. She had always hated plain water. But she loved Rhys, and he looked concerned, so she took a sip from the glass he was holding in front of her mouth. He smiled when she took a large gulp, and she waved him away. "Enough."

"I think you're dehydrated. That's what the nurse on the phone said."

"Just tired," she said, patting his arm and closing her eyes again.

A few minutes later she was wakened again—this time by a paramedic who insisted she come with them. They got her from the chair to the stretcher and then to the ambulance. She closed her eyes again, feeling thankful that she could at least rest until she arrived at the hospital.

CHAPTER 5

*C*laudia pulled her VW Bug up in front of the hospital, paid for parking, and ran through the emergency room entrance. Rhys was in the waiting area. "They told me I couldn't come in," he said. "She's bad. Is she going to die?"

She frowned at him and pulled him into a hug so he wouldn't see the panic she was feeling. "Let's get facts before we freak out, okay?"

"When I got to her house, she was so muddled. I don't even think she knew who I was."

"You said she might have been dehydrated. They'll probably just give her an IV to get some fluids into her.

Maybe keep her in overnight. Sit down. I'll be back soon."

He sat back down and took out his phone. "I should tell Mom."

"Have you told her anything yet?"

He looked at the man next to him and then back at her. "No, we wanted to wait until I knew more."

"Let's do that." She glanced over at the man who was seated near Rhys. "Clint? Is that you?"

"Oh, yeah," said Rhys. "Clint drove me here, helped me check on Grandma. He was waiting outside the door when I got there after practice."

What was Clint doing here? Claudia hadn't seen him since high school. Not since he had left her to travel the world. She looked at the man who had once been hers and remembered the laughter, the fun, and the heartbreak all in one tsunami of memory. She teetered a moment on her feet and grabbed at the arm of Clint's chair.

"It's probably just dehydration, but the paramedics were concerned enough to bring her in," said Clint, looking at her with an odd expression. "Are you okay?"

"I'm fine. I'll go see how she's doing." *And get out of your orbit*, she thought. Clint had always had a way of pulling her to him, like she was a planet seeking its sun. That he affected her this way, even after all these years, was unsettling.

"I'll wait here with Rhys."

Rhys nodded in acknowledgement then bowed over his phone, immediately engaged in a texting conversation. Or maybe he was scrolling social media. Whatever it was, he was now distracted.

"Go ahead," Clint said, smiling at his charge's short attention. "I really don't mind waiting."

A nurse at reception buzzed her into the treatment area. When she drew the curtain aside at bay three, her eyes lighted on a woman with a gray pallor who was sunk against the stark white pillow. Her white hair was unkempt, flattened, and her thin arm was attached to a tube that led to a bag of clear liquid just above her bed.

"Sorry," she mumbled. "Wrong room."

She let the curtain fall, and was about to go back to the nurses' station, when a small voice said, "Claudia?" She opened the curtain again. The woman's eyes were now open, and she was searching the room.

She stared in shock at the woman, whose gaze was glassy and confused.

"Oh, Mom." She stepped toward the bed. "Why didn't you tell me?"

"Claudia?" the woman asked uncertainly. "What are you doing here? Where is Karen?"

"Karen is in Mexico, remember? I told you I was coming."

"When?"

Claudia's heart fluttered in panic. How did she not remember their conversation from only two hours before?

"Mom, how are you feeling?" she asked in a soft voice, trying not to let anger overtake her. How could Karen not tell her how badly their mother was doing? For that matter, how could she just take off to Mexico and leave their mother alone? When her sister returned, Claudia would give her an earful.

"I'm tired," her mother said.

"Has the doctor been in to speak with you?" Claudia scanned her mother more closely now. She was thin, so much more so than when Claudia had visited in early

October. Had she not been eating? She looked no larger than a ten-year-old. As her grandmother used to say, one good wind would blow her away.

Claudia scanned the panel on the machine above her mother's bed, trying to make sense of the numbers flashing on the screen. One seemed to monitor her heart rate and another her blood oxygen levels. For a crazy minute, she wished she had gone into nursing like her sister and mother, instead of pursuing a career in social services. Where was Karen when she needed her?

"Doctor?" her mother asked, confused.

"You're in the hospital, Mom. The emergency room."

"I don't need to be here." Her mother put her hands onto the bed and tried to lever herself up.

Claudia rushed forward and gently put her hands on her mother's shoulders, urging her to stay where she was. "It's okay. I know how you hate the hospital. But we just want to make sure you're okay."

"I'm fine." Her mother smiled weakly, trying to placate, but Claudia knew that strategy well. Denial might as well have been her mother's middle name.

"Mom, this is no time for your stiff-upper-lip tactics." Her mother's way of brushing things off as unimportant was probably the reason she was here. "You need help, and we're staying here until you get it."

"They just poke and prod," said her mother, but Claudia noticed her settling back into the bed without further protest.

"You were a nurse. You know why they poke and prod. The test results will make it easier to make a diagnosis."

"Doesn't keep the inevitable from happening."

"Mom!"

"I brought your father in, and even once they diagnosed him, there wasn't anything they could do."

Tears welled up in Claudia's eyes as she thought of her poor father lying in this same hospital not a year earlier. She felt his loss every day. How must it be for her mother? Especially since Karen wasn't visiting every day anymore.

She took her mother's hand and held it between hers. "Mom, we all miss Dad so much, but he would want you to find a way to move forward, find things to enjoy in life."

"Ha," her mother said humorlessly. "As if that's possible."

"I'm not saying to forget him. I would never suggest that. But maybe you need to find something every day to look forward to. Or at least to be grateful for."

"Spare me the platitudes," her mother mumbled. But her voice was a little stronger now. "You're still young. You can't know what it's like to go through a loss like this. I hope you never do."

"I would have to have a love like yours and Dad's before that could happen," said Claudia.

"What about Alex? I thought you were happy with him." Her mother's eyes were sharper now, trained on her as though Claudia were five years old again and she was trying to uncover where Claudia had hidden her sister's toy.

She smiled though her teary eyes. "Alex is great. I just don't think he wants what I want."

"What do you want?"

"I want…" But she was interrupted by a young woman in scrubs with a name on her nameplate that Claudia could neither spell nor pronounce.

"Hello, I'm Dr. A. How are we doing?"

"I don't want to be prodded and poked," said her mother, gesturing with her chin to the tubes coming out of her arms. Claudia smiled an apology to the doctor.

"Thank you for your patience, Mrs. Woolf," said Dr. A. "Things are busy as always around here. But I have your test results." She pointed to the clipboard she was carrying. "It looks like you haven't been drinking enough fluids perhaps. Is there a reason for that?"

"I'm just not thirsty."

"Hmm," said the doctor, turning her gaze on Claudia. "And you are…?"

"Her daughter."

"I see. And do you get by to see your mother often?" Her tone made the question sound like an interrogation, and Claudia felt the sudden need to defend herself.

"No. I live in Vancouver. My sister, who lives in town, is on vacation, so she asked me to come and stay with

Mom. I arrived in town less than an hour ago. I haven't even been to the house yet."

"I see." Doctor A turned toward her patient again. "Mrs. Woolf, do you live alone?"

Her mother nodded.

"And do you get out to see friends very often?"

"Sometimes," said her mother.

"Tell me, what is your typical day like?"

Vivian sighed. "I get up at nine or ten. I make myself some lunch. Then I watch some TV or sometimes go for a walk."

"When do you see others?"

"On Fridays, my housekeeper comes to clean my bathrooms and the kitchen. And on Monday I put out the garbage. Sometimes I see people when I'm out pulling a weed out of the garden. And Karen visits most Sundays."

"Do you play bridge or pickleball or such?"

"Ned hates those games," she said.

"Ned?" Doctor A looked at her mother, who was now crying, and then turned to Claudia for clarification.

"Ned was my father. He passed away in January." Claudia grabbed a tissue from a box on a nearby shelf and, wishing it were softer, handed it to her mother.

"I see," said the doctor, and she marked something down on the clipboard. "Thank you. Excuse me; I will be back shortly."

Claudia left her mother's bedside and hurried after the doctor. "What's wrong? She's going to be okay, isn't she?"

Dr. A motioned for Claudia to join her near the nurse's station. "Your mother has severe dehydration, so I plan to keep her in overnight to make sure her kidneys haven't been compromised. I have requested a bed on a ward upstairs so she can get a decent sleep. But the underlying cause of the dehydration is what I am most concerned about."

"What do you mean?"

"I'm afraid your mother may be suffering from depression, probably brought on by your father's death. This time of year, is often hard for people anyway, and even more so for those who have a recent loss of the magnitude of losing a spouse. It sounds as though he was with you last year."

"Yes, we were all together. Even my brother and his family came from New Brunswick for Christmas last year."

"I expect this Christmas will be very hard for your mother. Especially if it's traditionally a special time of year for your family. The holidays remind people of family and love and belonging. But for the many people who are alone, this is a very lonely time of year. It is good that you're here."

"What can I do?"

"Well, I can suggest a few books and resources. There is a mental health agency you can consult. They have an excellent website. And I will recommend she see a specialist. Meanwhile, she should talk to her family doctor about it. There may be some medications she can take that will help. But what she really needs is activity, friends, people who care about her. And exercise. I'm concerned she is not getting out much."

"She recently fell and has been recovering from that," said Claudia. "I didn't know how serious it was."

"I recommend you take her to her regular physician as soon as you can. I believe it to be urgent, and if someone can check in with her frequently in the meantime, it would be best."

"Okay. I can do that." It gave her some relief to have some action she could take. Feeling helpless and sidelined was not Claudia's preference.

"I have left the request for a bed for your mother. As soon as we have one, we will transfer her upstairs."

"Can my nephew come in to see her in the meantime? He's the one who called the ambulance, and he's very anxious to see her."

"Of course. I'm told you may not need to wait too long for the bed, and we will probably only keep her for twenty-four to forty-eight hours. She should be physically well enough to be discharged by then." Dr. A emphasized the word *physically*.

Claudia thanked her before heading to the waiting room to call Rhys. Clint, who was still there watching sports highlights on the television, said he would wait longer in case they needed something. Then she and Rhys went back to see her mother, who was now dry-eyed.

Vivian smiled when she saw her grandson. "Hello, my dear. I'm sorry to have worried you."

"Hi, Grandma." Rhys went over to hug her. "You look better than you did a couple of hours ago."

Claudia cringed inwardly. If this was noticeably better, no wonder the kid had been scared.

She listened to the pair talk. Rhys told her about band practice and made her promise to come to the concert on the twentieth.

"I wouldn't miss it for the world," said her mother, perking up at the invitation. Maybe the doctor was right. Her mother had been alone too much this year, and she needed some company and tender loving care.

Her phone rang, and she looked down at the screen. "It's Karen."

"Don't tell her about this," her mother warned. "I don't want her holiday to be interrupted for my sake."

Claudia and Rhys exchanged glances, and she answered the call.

"So are you there?" asked her sister without even bothering to say hello.

"Yes. I just got here about an hour ago."

"And how's Rhys? Did he come home too?"

"Rhys is fine. Do you want to talk to him?" He looked at her and waved his hands in protest. That was a no.

"No, don't bother him. I just want to know why he hasn't been answering my texts."

She put her hand over the phone and whispered, "She wants to know why you aren't answering her texts."

"Tell her the phone died," whispered Rhys.

"It seems his phone died. We're going to take a quick drive over to your place to pick up his charger."

"What about Mom?"

"Mom?"

"How is she?"

Claudia pointed at the phone and at her mother to ask if she wanted to speak to her. Her mother shook her head no. What was it about this family and their secrets?

"Mom's in bed right now. She seems tired, so I figure she has a lot on. You know how December is." She looked at her mother then and wished she had said nothing. The doctor was right. This was going to be a horrible Christmas unless she could find some way to inject some joy. "I'll get her to send you an email tomorrow when she has some time."

"Yes, that would be good. Thanks." Her sister's voice was buzzing in her ear, and she forced herself to pay attention. "Give them a hug then," said Karen. "And thanks for coming. I knew I could count on you."

"You didn't give me much of a choice," she said. "Next time I would appreciate some notice."

"I'm sorry about that. But Mom told me not to say anything. You know how she can be."

Claudia eyed her mother, who was happily chatting with Rhys at the other end of the room, looking much more alert than she had only ten minutes earlier. "Yes, I do. I should go. I just got in and I still have some work to do tonight." After her sister said goodbye, she hung up and looked at her mother. She couldn't believe she had just taken part in this subterfuge. At least she now understood why Karen had said nothing about their mother's fall.

"Does Blaine know you fell?" She asked her mother as

she approached the bed to sit down on the chair on the side opposite Rhys.

"Of course not. I don't want to worry your brother over something so trivial."

"Right." She wasn't surprised by her mother's response, but it made her feel guilty. She had promised Blaine she would keep him up to date on their mother's progress, and she had trusted Karen to tell her. Now it was clear that her mother was either telling Karen not to bother them with news or she was good at masking. From now on, she wouldn't stay in the dark anymore. She would have to come and see her mother at least once a month. And this month, she would stay for the rest of December and into the new year. She just needed to square it with her boss.

But how would they make it through the next three weeks? She thought of her father and the fun he always brought to the season. He had been like a tall lanky Santa, always laughing, taking them on Christmas-light tours and sleigh rides, bringing them to festivals, whatever was on offer. And he always sent her mother presents, one a day for the twelve days before Christmas, starting on the fourteenth.

Oh, no. How could she have forgotten that tradition? When December fourteenth rolled around and Dad's small gift was missing, her mother would be devastated. She'd have to think of something to distract her, but not today. Today she just wanted to get something to eat and get to bed.

A nurse came into the treatment area, followed by an orderly. Claudia motioned for Rhys to step aside so they could move her mom to the gurney.

"We'll see you in the morning, Mom," she said, bending to kiss her mother's cheek.

"Have a good sleep, Grandma." Her mother patted Rhys's hand, and as they wheeled her away, she had a genuine smile on her face, with only a trace of the melancholy she had carried since her husband's death.

Claudia stood next to Rhys, waving, watching them wheel her away, and remembering the last time she had said goodbye in this hospital. That goodbye had been final. Forcing down tears, she turned to Rhys.

"Have you eaten?"

"No. I was supposed to grab a pizza with the guys after practice, but after you called, I just booted it over there."

"I'm glad you did."

"Me too. She was in rough shape. Do you think she should live in a home?"

A home? Her strong, independent mother didn't belong in a home. Then again, she was in the hospital because she hadn't been drinking enough water. Maybe Rhys knew more than she did.

"Do you think she should be in a home?" she asked.

"Mom thinks so."

"Really?"

"I heard her talking to Dad about it," Rhys said gravely. "She said that she wanted to get Grandma to give up her house and move to a smaller place. Said that maybe a retirement community would be best." His perpetual smile was now turned down. It was hard to see him like that. Rhys was always such a cheerful kid. But as Claudia looked up at him, she realized he wasn't a kid anymore. Six feet at least. And he had a shadow on his chin and a shock of black hair that fell over one eye. No, Rhys was not a boy anymore. He was a young man.

She reached out and patted him on the arm. "If I understand you correctly, she's probably talking about one of those condos where people over fifty-five live. Not an extended care unit." At least she hoped not. She had done some volunteer work in one of those a few years before, for social work practicum. Her mother didn't belong there. As far as she was concerned, that entire system needed to be overhauled.

"But your mother may have a point. A year ago, I wouldn't have thought Grandma would need to move at all. I guess I always imagined her staying in her house with your grandpa. But now that he's gone, it may be too much for one person. She's just not herself."

"I wish she would be her old self," said Rhys. "I miss *that* grandma."

"Well, she certainly brightened up when you came in the room."

"Yeah?" he asked, his frown disappearing into a grin. "I'm glad about that. She did seem better than when I found her."

"And I am so grateful you did find her," said Claudia. "Now, let's go and get some dinner. You must be starved."

When they got back to the waiting room, Clint stood and walked over to them.

"How's she doing?" he asked. He was close now, and she found herself having to look up at him too. He had filled out since high school and now sported a thick auburn beard that complemented his wavy hair. He was taller than she remembered, and his physical presence dominated the room. She took a half step back before answering him, struggling to gain her equilibrium.

"They're keeping her in for observation," she said. "It's a good thing you two found her. She was severely dehydrated, as you suspected."

"It happened to my mother a few times," said Clint.

"I was sorry to hear she passed," she said. "How is your dad doing?"

"It's been a few years, so he's learned to cope. Listen, I would love to catch up, but can we do it over a meal? I haven't had dinner yet."

"Neither have I," said Rhys.

"What do you two suggest?"

"Pizza," said Rhys. "Mom hates it, so whenever she's away my dad and I usually grab one."

"Sounds great," said Clint. "I'll meet you at the one

near the college. Angelo's. It's a little farther, but it's still the best in town."

It was also where he used to take her when they were going out together in high school. But she would ignore that tiny fact, because she was hungry too—and Angelo's pizza really was the best in town.

CHAPTER 6

*R*hys and Claudia walked out to the parking lot and climbed into her red VW. Soon she was squinting in the darkness, trying to get her bearings as she drove out of the parking lot.

"I'll need you to direct me. There's been a lot of construction here the past few years. I'm not sure where I'm going."

"Turn left at the road, and after about five blocks, turn left again."

She followed his directions and soon saw the restaurant on the right-hand side of the road, the *open* sign still brightly lit.

"How do you know Clint?" asked Rhys.

"We went to high school together," she said. "But I haven't seen him since I graduated. He went traveling for a year, and I stayed to help Mom with my grandmother, who suffered a stroke a month before I graduated."

"Where was my mom?"

"Karen was working at the hospital in Victoria. And she had a two-year-old, if I'm not mistaken.

"Jessie?"

"No, Jess would have been five by then. The two-year-old was you."

"How many years did you help with your grandmother?"

"She died five years later, so then I finished my degree and moved to the city."

"Mom never told me that," said Rhys. "I thought you moved right after high school and went to university in Vancouver."

"Nope. I did my first degree here. Then I went on to get a master's in Vancouver. Anyway, Cint and I used to date in high school, but I haven't seen him since we graduated. I heard he married a girl in Australia. Maybe even had kids, but I'm not sure."

She was positive. The summer after Clint left town, a friend of his had told her that Clint was getting married and having a child. He had left her forever, and a piece of her heart had never been the same since.

"And you met Alex," said Rhys. "He's a great guy."

"Yes, Alex is a nice guy."

*S*he pulled into the parking lot, and they got out. Rhys walked ahead, held open the door for her, and when they entered, he looked around the room, then smiled and waved at one of the servers and a few of the patrons.

"So your mother goes away often?" she asked.

"What?" He turned toward her as though he'd forgotten she was there. "No. Why do you ask?"

"You seem to know a lot of the people here. I thought maybe you were a regular."

He blushed. "I come here sometimes after school," he said. "My girlfriend works here."

She looked up at the server, a young woman with dark hair piled high on her head in a messy bun. She frowned at Claudia. "Hi, Rhys. I didn't expect you to be here today."

"Wasn't planning to be here, but we were just up at the hospital with Grandma. Cam, this is my Aunt Claudia. Claudia, this is my girlfriend, Cam." He was blushing again, and Claudia bit back a smile when she saw the relief on the young woman's face. She should have been flattered, she supposed, that a sixteen-year-old girl who looked twenty-two was even remotely jealous. Claudia felt well beyond her years most days.

"What happened to your grandma?" asked Cam.

"Dehydrated," said Rhys. "But she's looking a lot better, isn't she, Claudia?"

"Much better," said Claudia. "But we missed dinner because of the madness. Could we get a table for three, please?" And, right on cue, the door opened and Clint walked in. His father came in behind him. "Make that a table for four," she said.

They followed Cam to a booth near the back of the pizzeria, and she set down menus and left to bring them some water—and a soda for Rhys. Claudia watched him bloom under her gaze. *Ah, young love.* Wasn't it grand?

"Hi, Mr. Jones," Claudia said as they settled in. "We're glad you could join us."

"I called Dad to let him know I would be later, and he insisted on coming to hear firsthand about your mother," Clint said.

"As I told Clint," Mr. Jones said, nodding to his son, "I promised Ned I would watch over her. This was in the hospital, just before he passed. Though she is difficult to watch over. She's been so withdrawn… and, since summer ended, I barely see her. Besides, I feel responsible for her fall."

"You shouldn't have agreed to watch Neville," said Clint. "That dog is a handful." His father frowned at him and shook his head.

"You may meet Neville," Mr. Jones said to Claudia. "Cute dog, but he's an escape artist. He belongs to Joe's son, but he and his wife travel in November and December every year to do their volunteer work. So Neville stays here."

"I'm not sure I remember Joe," said Claudia. "Where does he live?"

"He's the neighbor on the other side of your mother. His partner is Helen, a good friend of your mom's. She and Joe are stuck in Toronto because of a big snowstorm that closed the airport. Their flights were canceled, and they aren't sure how long it will take to get back from their trip to the Bahamas. They were supposed to catch their connecting flight yesterday."

"That is bad luck," said Claudia. She noticed Rhys's girlfriend watching their table. "We should probably decide on our order so Cam can get it started."

They quickly decided on a Hawaiian pizza for Rhys and Clint and a vegetable-and-beef option for Tom and Claudia.

"How is your mother?" Tom asked, after Cam had taken their order. "When you phoned, I sent Clint over to bang on the door, but she didn't answer. Thank goodness you came along, young fella." Tom smiled at Rhys.

"I am concerned about her," said Claudia. "She's not eating or drinking enough. She looks at least ten pounds lighter than she did when I visited her on Labor Day weekend, and my mother already weighs less than a bird."

"She misses your father," said Tom. "I know how hard it can be to lose your spouse." His voice cracked a little, and he busied himself adding some cream to the coffee he'd ordered.

"But you're doing well now, Dad. You've got your woodshop projects, and you're teaching woodworking to a couple of guys. You still go to the pool a few times a week, and you're always out walking." Clint numbered off his father's activities on his fingers.

"That's true," said Tom. "But it hasn't been easy. I miss your mother every single day."

"You were married a long time," said Claudia.

"Forty-nine years," he said wistfully, then took a sip of the coffee that was now well and truly stirred.

"How did you get through your first year without her?" she asked. "Do you have any tips?"

They all turned toward him, and Tom pushed himself to the back of the booth as though he might want to run away. Then he said, "Your dad. I owe him for that."

"Dad? What did he do?"

"Well, he came around every day for the first several months. Listened to me go on and on about Marge and gradually convinced me to come out with him for a walk, and then to the pool, and then to the Men's Shack downtown, where they do woodworking projects. It got me back into wood turning, and I started making things. I'm not sure what I would have done without your dad. He was a true friend. I wish I could help Vivian like he helped me."

The pizza arrived, and Rhys and Clint dove in first. She watched them consume two pieces each before taking a piece for herself.

"This really is the best pizza," she said, after taking her first bite.

Tom took a bite as well, and hummed in agreement.

"I think Mom is depressed," she said after her third bite. "And I'm really worried about this month. Especially since their 'Twelve Days of Christmas' tradition would normally start next week."

"What's that?" Clint asked.

"Grandpa always gave Grandma a present every day for twelve days, with the largest present on Christmas Day," explained Rhys.

"We need something to distract her from that," said Claudia. "I thought about taking her away a few months ago, but she doesn't want to go anywhere."

"It would only postpone the inevitable," said Tom. "Next year he's still going to be gone."

Claudia nodded, feeling tears dangerously close to forming.

"Maybe we can send her gifts from us instead?" Rhys suggested.

"That might work," said Claudia.

"It could," said Tom. "But if you want my opinion, I think it would be better to try to start a new tradition."

"Yeah," said Rhys, around a bite of pizza. "And find a way to get her out of the house. All she does is sit in the recliner chair and stare at the pear tree."

"Really?"

"It's where I found her tonight. She had fallen asleep looking out the window. We need to get her to go outside."

"Or at least get her *wanting* to go outside," said Tom before taking up his second piece of pizza. "This really is good. We should come here more often, Clint."

"I've always loved this place," said Clint, looking at Claudia. Was he remembering their times here, too? She blushed and quickly grabbed her purse from beside her. "I'm just going to use the facilities," she said, scooting Rhys out of the booth so she could get away.

When she got to the bathroom, she pulled out her phone to see if Alex had sent a message to at least acknowledge that he got her note.

Nothing. So he was still mad about their disagreement this morning. Well, she was going to take the high road, so she texted him quickly. *I made it to my mom's place. Sorry about this morning. Hope you are okay.*

She hesitated a moment before adding, *Love you.* And then she wondered, not for the first time that month, whether saying it had just become a habit. Because with Clint so close, making her remember the wonder and excitement of her first love, she wasn't sure anymore.

At least she had an excuse to avoid her relationship troubles, she thought as she returned to the table. Her first priority was to help her mother, because in a very real sense, Vivian's quality of life depended on it.

They finished the pizza soon after and left the restaurant. "Tom and I have been talking about Grandma. He says he'll think about how to get her out more," said Rhys. "But we do have some ideas."

"What kind of ideas?" asked Claudia.

The three men looked at each other. "Well," said Clint, "Dad says that if your mother is withdrawn, it may help to get her out to do things she used to enjoy."

"One of those things is the Community Tree Festival," said Tom. "She usually bakes quite a bit for it, and spends time at the baking table during that weekend."

"That's right. How long has that been happening, now?"

"It's the festival's twenty-fifth anniversary this year, and I think we could convince her not to miss it. She and your father were two of the founders of the event."

"I remember that," said Claudia. "I'll see how she's feeling when she gets out tomorrow. I can help her with the baking."

"We also need to decorate the house," said Rhys. "We always have Christmas dinner with Gran and Gramps, but the house isn't even decorated yet."

"We can head out tomorrow after school and pick up a tree if you like," said Claudia.

"Mom and Dad aren't even coming home until the twenty-second. How about I just bring over our fake tree?"

"That's a good idea. You sure your mother won't want to decorate?"

"Not if we decorate Grandma's place. She hates getting things ready for Christmas. It's Grandpa who loved to decorate."

"I can pick you up after school, and we can probably strap it to the roof of the car."

Rhys laughed. "I'm not sure it's big enough, Claudia."

"I have a truck, if it will help," offered Clint. "Rhys and I can swing by after I get home from work tomorrow."

Claudia looked at him a moment, wary of accepting the help if it meant spending more time with him. Clint was wearing his slow smile, the one that could knock a woman off-balance. That *of-course-you'll-let-me-help-you* look always made her feel one part defensive and one part puddle of feelings.

But it would be easier than trying to strap a Christmas tree box to her tiny roof. Besides, she'd probably have to work late tomorrow, especially if she took time out to visit or gather her mother from the hospital.

"Thank you. That would be really helpful," she said finally.

"Rhys, why don't you give me your number?" Clint handed his cell to Rhys, who entered his phone number into his contacts. "I'll send you a text when I'm ready to go."

"That's great," said Rhys.

"Do you happen to know what else my mother enjoyed doing before she lost Dad?" Claudia asked Tom.

He nodded. "She and Marge, my wife, used to knit a fair bit. I think they belonged to the same knitting guild." He paused. "And she used to be part of a walking club too. Marge couldn't go with her much just before she passed. She lost her mobility early." Tom frowned, lost in memories for a moment. "They used to help at the community center, though—spent a lot of time there, especially with the new mothers. Your mom had a hard time letting go of nursing."

"I didn't know that."

"Talk to Helen when she gets back. She would be able to tell you about more recent interests. I believe we need to force her to stop focusing on herself if she's going to feel better."

"Do you really think that will work?" asked Claudia.

Tom nodded slowly. "People, exercise, giving to a cause bigger than oneself, creative expression… That's what got me through my first few years after losing Marge. If your father hadn't made me get out, I would still be sitting in front of the television, wasted away to nothing by now. I owe it to him to help Vivian find her feet again too."

"So we have knitting, baking, decorating the house," Claudia said, counting on her fingers. "Anything else?'

"Your mother is also an excellent host. Maybe we should plan a Christmas celebration at her house this year. In honor of Ned," Tom added. "He wouldn't want to see her this way."

"That's a great idea," said Claudia.

"And don't forget to ask Helen to help," said Tom. "I know she's been worried about her."

"Helen might be able to convince her to hold a party," said Claudia. "Mom doesn't listen to me, but if her friend asks her, we might have better luck."

"Joe said he and Helen were trying to get tickets for three days from now. It's fortunate Helen has family in Toronto they can stay with."

"Yes, I can't imagine hanging out in the Toronto airport for too long. Especially with all those people." Claudia shivered just thinking about it. She turned to Rhys. "You and Clint are going to get the tree so we can decorate the house, and if your grandma balks at it, I'm putting you in charge of convincing her it's a good idea. She can't say no to you." She remembered how her mother's face had lit up when Rhys came into the hospital room. "And I'll talk to Helen about convincing her to have a party."

"I'll give it some thought," said Tom. "I'm sure there are other ways to get her out and about. She'll be so busy this season it will get her out of herself again."

"I feel like we should be putting our hands in and calling out a cheer," said Rhys, laughing.

"Why not?" Claudia put her hand out. "Go, Project Vivian!" They put their hands into the circle and cheered, then said good night and dispersed to their cars.

"I hope this helps," said Rhys. "She's been really sad."

"I wish I had known how bad she was," said Claudia. She would have made the effort to come home more often. She could have come to the island on Alex's monthly visits to see his parents, and they could have driven down here before heading home. Instead, she had stayed home. Worked. Told herself that after she got the promotion things would slow down.

"Mom didn't seem too worried," said Rhys. "And I've been busy with the bands and courses. So I've only been over a few times. Maybe if we had visited her more often… But she kept saying, 'You're busy, I'm fine,' so we mostly phoned her."

"You mean your mom didn't visit every week?" She remembered her mother saying Karen came for a weekly visit. Had she been lying? Or even stretching the truth?

"Mom used to phone her pretty much daily, even when Grandpa was alive." Rhys's voice cracked a little with emotion. "Until she fell, I don't think either of us had been there for weeks."

"I had no idea." Claudia mentally kicked herself for refusing to come with Alex on those occasions he had visited the island. Until she spoke to Karen, she wouldn't know how often her mother had company, outside of the cleaning service. Maybe it was time to put her mother into a facility so she would be safe.

She would speak to Karen soon. But at the moment she felt nothing but anger toward her sister. How could she not take the time to visit, at least once every two weeks?

When they returned to her mother's place, Claudia carried her things from her car to the second guest room upstairs. She had never lived in this house, but she had stayed here plenty of times over the past twenty-five years. The guest rooms were both comfortable, but she preferred this one. It was small and quiet, with a desk overlooking the backyard. She could work or sleep without being interrupted much.

She looked over at the queen-sized bed, decorated with a plush duvet and soft feather pillows, and sighed.

She missed Alex.

She pulled her phone out of her purse. He hadn't texted her back. Not unusual, as he wasn't attached at the hip to his telephone like she was, but he could have at least said hello and asked her how her mother was doing. He should be able to set aside their differences long enough to accomplish that.

Then again, she ruminated as she descended the stairs to see how Rhys was doing, they rarely disagreed like they had that morning. He hadn't told her about family law—she was pretty sure she would remember that. What type of job had he applied for? And why had he chosen that morning to spring it on her?

"Hey," she said to Rhys, who was sitting on the couch, concentrating on his laptop. "You okay? You need anything?"

He looked up, startled. "Yeah, I mean no. I'm good. I was just chilling for a few minutes, then I'll go to my room. I usually stay in the basement."

"The one your mom used to sleep in." Claudia sat in the chair opposite him, her elbows on her knees. "I used to be so jealous that she got that room while I had to sleep upstairs outside Mom's room."

"Yeah?" he asked, his fingers flying across the keyboard. "Why's that?"

"Because she got away with more than I did. But she *was* seven years older, so I suppose our parents though I would be better off upstairs. Then my grandma moved in after her stroke, so I never did get that room." She smiled wryly. Though she had spent plenty of nights on the main-floor sofa, listening for her grandmother. She felt she had to because of the distance between the basement and the upstairs. Someone had to listen for Grandma, and because her mother and father both worked full-time, it fell to her. She was only working a few days a week and going to school.

"Uh-huh," said Rhys, without looking up from the screen.

Claudia rose again and walked over to put her hand on his shoulder. "Don't stay up too late. You have that test in the morning."

He looked up at her and smiled a ghost of a smile. "I'll be ready," he said, so she walked back up to her room and changed into pajamas.

She looked at the right side of the bed where Alex usually slept, and climbed into the left-hand side. She turned out the light and, in the dark, imagined that just for tonight she could get back what she and Alex seemed to have lost in the past few months.

As she closed her eyes, she heard Clint outside yelling, "Neville, you get back here!" His voice was deep and warm, even in anger, and she went to sleep dreaming of days past.

And knowing that nothing was ever going to be the same again.

CHAPTER 7

*R*hys was up early and crashing around the kitchen when Claudia padded downstairs.

"What's going on?"

"She has no food," he said.

Claudia opened the door and looked inside. "There are eggs, bread, vegetables."

"Those are ingredients." He huffed. "I need food. I gotta be at school in an hour for my math exam."

Claudia smiled. Her sister was right. Though Rhys had taken charge the night before and acted as adult as anyone twice his age, he still needed to be taken care of when it came to some things.

"Do you like omelets?"

"Yes."

"Broccoli? Cheese? Spinach? Onions?"

"No onions. Cam hates it when I eat them."

"No onions, then." She took out the ingredients, and then found a frying pan and some olive oil in the cupboard.

"Grab me a plate, will you?" she said over her shoulder. "And pop a couple pieces of bread in the toaster oven."

"Sure," he said, opening the package of bread.

"What do you usually drink in the morning?"

"Orange juice. Or coffee."

"Do you know how to make coffee?"

"No."

"No time like the present to learn." She pointed out the machine and told him to find some coffee filters and a package of ground coffee. "I think it's in the cupboard above the machine."

He opened the cupboard doors and pulled out what she asked for. Then she told him how to put the filter in, measure out the coffee, and fill the machine with water. He followed her instructions to the letter, and within a few minutes the aroma of fresh coffee filled the kitchen. The toaster oven dinged, and she watched him butter the toast.

She slid the omelet she'd prepared onto a plate and placed it on the island. Rhys poured two cups of coffee and sat down. "This looks great," he said, diving in. "Can you show me how to make one? Mom never has time. I don't want to go to university and only know how to make packaged noodles. I don't even like them."

"Sure." She smiled. "I can show you how to cook. But you know who the best cook is in this family?"

He looked up at her, his brow furrowed, and then he smiled. "Grandma."

"I bet if you asked her, she might help you, too."

"And it would give her something else to do that she likes," said Rhys, taking a bite of his toast. "Like we were talking about last night."

"Exactly. You can use the excuse that your mother promised to teach you but hasn't had time."

"Genius!"

Claudia laughed at his enthusiasm. "You'd better eat up or you'll be late. Do you need me to drop you anywhere?"

"No, I want to walk to school with Cam. She just lives up the street." He shoveled the next few bites into his mouth, finished his coffee, nearly chucked his dishes in the dishwasher, then rushed out of the house, putting Claudia in mind of a tornado.

Claudia walked through the house. It was the first time she had seen it in daylight in months. She cringed a little as she walked from room to room, wondering which rooms the house cleaner normally paid attention to—because it was obviously not the guest rooms, the office, or her mother's bedroom.

Unopened mail was piled high on the study desk, dishes were scattered around the house, and the bed hadn't been made. There were dust bunnies multiplying under the beds, and a thin film of dust covered most of the surfaces in the other rooms.

Why hadn't Karen told her what was happening? Or perhaps she had. Claudia thought back on their conversations in recent months but concluded that no, Karen hadn't said anything.

Maybe she didn't know. Karen wasn't much of a cook, so she would rarely go into the kitchen. And if she was coming only on Sundays, and the house cleaner came on Fridays, she might not think anything was amiss. The front room, where her mother took company— including, presumably, Karen—seemed to be one of the only rooms that had received attention.

Claudia returned to her room and opened her laptop to see if there were any urgent queries, and she checked to see if Alex had responded yet.

Nothing.

Did that mean she would soon be on her own? If he left, they would have to sell their condo. Though they had some equity in it, affording anything on her own would be difficult.

She would have to find a place to rent, and that meant living further out of town. So Alex would get what he wanted whether she wanted it or not. She would have to give up her easy commute—or possibly a job she loved —just because he felt like he was being left behind. Just because he wanted to change their lives without so much as a by-your-leave.

Maybe he was having a midlife crisis. Though he was only forty-three, he had been telling her for a while about how his friends were moving on with their lives, trying new things, having kids, traveling, all while he was working for the same law firm, doing the same corporate contracts for the same companies.

He had told her he was tired of it, but after a while, she told him to stop complaining. If he wanted it to change, he should do something about it.

And he had stopped complaining. She remembered her relief at not having to hear the same old concerns every night. It had allowed her to focus on other things. But now it seemed he had taken her at her word. He was doing something about it, and had been for over a year.

Maybe the job wasn't the only thing he was tired of. If he wanted to move when he knew she had just started a job she had worked so hard for, maybe that was his way of breaking up. Maybe he didn't see a future with her anymore.

And maybe that feeling was mutual.

She scowled at her unanswered messages and put the phone away. She had to stop thinking about Alex, so she headed to the shower to dress and then returned to her desk to answer some emails for work, surprised there were so few now that she had acquired approval for the project she had been championing.

Once she handed it over to a contract manager, she was free to oversee it as part of her portfolio, but it was a relief not to be so involved in the day-to-day details anymore. It freed up her time to look at more strategic questions, like the best direction for the organization to take in the coming year.

For that, she needed to examine board minutes, reports about what the organization had achieved, and other data, and complete an analysis so she could be prepared for the board meeting to be held in January. She also needed to talk to Khalid about his thoughts, so she buried herself in reading until her phone rang.

It was Alex. It was strange to hear from him at this time of day. Bracing herself for his good news about the interview, she answered the call.

"I am so sorry," said Alex as soon as she said hello. "I didn't see your note until Mom found it this morning."

"What? Your mom?" She was confused. "Aren't your parents in Hawaii?"

"They were. Then they were going to Ontario to my great-aunt's ninetieth birthday, remember? Anyway, their flight was canceled because of that storm. So now they're here for the next few days until they can get a flight. I didn't see your note, and I had forgotten my phone at the office. I was in such a hurry to pick them up from the airport."

Well, that explained that, she thought, feeling a little relieved that he hadn't just ignored her. Still, that didn't explain why he hadn't sent her an email or something.

"Didn't you wonder where I was?"

He didn't answer for a moment, then said in a whisper, "I thought you left me. Or had gone to stay with a friend for a day or two."

"Why would you think that?"

"Because you were angry yesterday, remember? And you said you didn't know if you would be home."

"If I was going to leave you, I wouldn't just walk out." What kind of person did he think she was? "We've been together for six years, Alex."

"I've never seen you so angry before. How was I supposed to know?"

"Because I tell you what I'm up to. I don't go off applying for jobs and changing my life plan without you. At least I haven't up until now."

It was a low blow, and she could already see the conversation spiraling into a new fight about the same topic, so she changed the subject. "How are your parents?"

"They're fine," he said, sounding relieved. "I'm calling to see how your mom is. You never told me she fell."

"I didn't know. Karen didn't tell me until yesterday, when she called from the airport." She caught him up on her mother's status and ended by saying, "I have permission to work from here for the next couple of weeks until my vacation starts. And I need to work on setting up a plan with my mother. She's not doing well. So I probably won't be home until after that."

"Of course," he said. "I'll come as soon as I get Mom and Dad on their way. Text me a list of things you need me to bring, and tell her I send my love."

"You don't have to; I know you're busy." Though right now, she wanted him to be there. To have him to lean on. Instead, she would have to do what she always did: lean on herself.

"Do you not want me to come?" he asked.

"No, it's not that. I would love you to come," she said, knowing a part of her was lying. Part of her wanted a break. But if they were going to work through this latest pitfall in their relationship, it was probably best to be in the same area code.

"As soon as I wrap things up at work, I'll be there. I have vacation from the twentieth on," he said. "It's been too long since we had some time together."

"I'm still working." She was feeling defensive, but she wasn't sure why.

"I know." The fatigue in his voice was palpable.

"You sound tired."

"I am, but it'll be better once I get my parents on their way and finish the file I'm working on."

"Try to get some rest in the meantime," she said.

"Yes." There was a long pause. "Did you give any more thought to what we talked about?"

"About you changing careers?"

"Yes," he said. "And moving."

"I haven't, but I've been kind of busy with Mom and work," she lied. The subject had been crisscrossing her mind like an army of ants, to the point where she could think of nothing else.

"I had the interview yesterday," he said offhandedly.

"How did it go?" She asked because she knew he expected her to. But she knew. If Alex wanted a job, he usually got it. His quintessential charm and positivity always won people over.

"They'll let me know in the next week or so. There are other candidates, and because I am new to the field, I'm at a disadvantage. But…"

"But you really want this," she said, her heart sinking.

"I know it's asking a lot of you," he said. "I know how hard you worked for that promotion."

Well, at least he was able to acknowledge what she would be losing.

"But maybe there are options," he continued. "Remote work is more common than it used to be." His voice was hopeful and, to her mind, overly optimistic. There was positive thinking, and then there was delusional thinking.

She shook her head. The organization had already insisted that those in management be on-site. She swallowed. If she wanted to keep him in her life, she would probably have to give up her job eventually. "We'll talk about it when you get here," she said. "When we can sit down and work it all through."

"Yes. Let's do that." He still sounded hopeful. "I have to go now. The client is coming in a few minutes."

"Okay," she said. "I'll talk to you later."

She heard him say "I love you" just before she hung up, and before she had a chance to say it back.

She stared at the phone and thought about how long it had been since they had spent any quality time together. She realized that, except for the occasional date night, it really had been almost a year since they'd really talked. Before her promotion, before her dad got sick. Before her whole world turned upside down.

No wonder it felt like they were growing apart. They had become nothing but roommates with very occasional benefits.

How could she have let that happen?

Turning back to her computer and opening her calendar, she considered what she needed to do that day. The first was to connect with her staff, so she pulled energy from inside herself, dialed into an online meeting, plastered a smile on her face, and faked some of Alex's positivity. She learned her team was doing a good job, judging from the updates she had received and the questions they were asking, which was helpful. With the rest of her life in such flux, at least something seemed to be working.

After her call, she worked until an alarm on her phone reminded her to call the hospital for an update. Feeling a little guilty that she hadn't thought of her mother all morning—so lost was she in worry about Alex's job possibilities—she dialed the hospital and asked for the nurse's station.

"Her doctor has hospital rounds in about an hour," the nurse told her. "Then she will either be kept in or discharged."

"How is she doing?"

"Your mother had a pretty good night," said the nurse.

"But it isn't clear how long she'll need to stay. We should know before noon."

"I'll come up then to see her," said Claudia. "Thank you."

She set her watch for another hour so she would remind herself to do just that. It wasn't unusual for her to become immersed in work and not come up for air until hours later. Alex was right about that. Though he was no better, really. How many days did he arrive home, well after nine, only to roll into bed, fall asleep, and rise again so he could be in the office by six thirty?

At twelve twenty, Claudia walked into her mother's hospital room to find her in conversation with her doctor. Good timing, she thought.

"Hello, dear," said her mother, beckoning her further into the room. "Doctor Kincaid was just telling me what they know so far. You may as well hear it. Then I won't have to tell you later."

"Hello, and you are…?" The doctor addressed her from over a pair of reading glasses.

"Claudia, Vivian's daughter."

"I didn't realize you had two daughters," said the doctor. "Usually Karen is here."

"Karen is taking a much-deserved vacation," said her mother, which reminded Claudia that she needed to focus on her mother instead of her own problems today.

"I was just about to tell your mother what we have learned," said the doctor, lifting the first few pages of his chart to scan the results underneath. "You were very low on fluids when you came in, Vivian. That put some strain on your organs, particularly the kidneys." His voice was grave, and Claudia's heart beat a little faster. How could this have happened? She would have to ask Karen when she'd last visited their mother and really paid attention.

"Is that something that can happen quickly?" she asked the doctor.

"Yes—in a matter of days, without enough fluids. It was good you brought her in when you did," he said, then turned toward her mother. "Vivian, I am wondering what you have been doing since your fall last week. At that time, we didn't notice anything to be concerned about."

"It's been hard to get up," she said. "So I stopped drinking water, so I didn't have to…" She blushed. "You know." She looked at Claudia beseechingly.

"You mean it hurt too much to get up and go to the washroom, so you stopped drinking?" asked Claudia.

"Yes." Her mother nodded.

"I wondered," said the doctor. "Just to be sure, I want to keep you in for another night to get your fluids up and stable. Then I will run another few tests in the morning to ensure you are on the mend. Is there anyone at home looking out for you?"

His eyes were on Claudia now, his expression expectant.

"Yes. I'm staying with Mom until she's able to be on her own again," said Claudia. "And until my sister gets back."

"Good." The doctor smiled. "Then I won't have concerns about releasing you tomorrow, provided your numbers are stable."

He left them alone, and Claudia looked at her mother, who a moment ago had been all smiles. She was now sunk deep in the pillow, her pallor still gray. It was as though the doctor had taken all her energy with him when he left. Her eyes had already begun to drift shut.

"How are you feeling today, Mom?" Claudia asked tentatively. She almost didn't want to hear the answer.

Her mother's eyes fluttered open again. "I'm bone-tired, Claudia. I just want to sleep."

"I'll let you do that, then," she said. "I'll come by later with Rhys to see how you are."

Her mother nodded almost imperceptibly, her eyes now completely shut. Claudia pulled the curtain around the bed to shut out some of the sunshine and tiptoed out of the room. She couldn't stay and watch her mother sleep. It was too hard to see her so thin and fragile. She told herself that her time would be better spent doing something constructive.

So she drove to the other end of town, returned to her laptop, let her boss know that she would be on the island for another week at least, and began delegating more work to her two managers. It would be a good test, she told herself, to see if they could handle the extra responsibility at a time when she could check in on them regularly for updates. Better to test them now than at a time when she wasn't available at all. If she decided to move, that time might be sooner than later.

At three o'clock, she shut down the computer, walked through the house to gauge what needed to be done, stripped her mother's bed, and collected dirty clothes and towels along the way. Laundry was an easy place to start. After throwing a load in, she went into the kitchen to do dishes and clear up the counters, then moved to the living room to dust and vacuum.

An hour and a half later, the house smelled of fabric softener and vinegar. She had swept, scrubbed, and dusted. And now she was hungry. Rhys would be home soon, so she began to chop vegetables and defrost some meat. Spaghetti would be easy, and teens all liked spaghetti. But Rhys was right about the food. By the time she was done, even the "ingredients" in the fridge were lacking. She would need to shop on her way home from visiting her mother at the hospital later that evening.

Rhys and Clint arrived with the tree just as Claudia was filling a saucepan with water for the pasta.

"Smells good," said Clint, setting the boxed tree in the foyer.

"You can join us if you like," she said, reaching for some more pasta to add to the pot.

"That would be great," he said, taking off his coat and hanging it up in the hall.

Rhys set the table, and they all sat down fifteen minutes later to a salad-and-spaghetti dinner. "This looks awesome, Claudia," said Rhys. "Can you teach me how to make this too?"

"Sure," she said, pleased by his enthusiasm. She rarely cooked for Alex anymore; by the time he got home, he had usually grabbed something on the way. At one time, she had really enjoyed cooking. When had that changed?

"How's Grandma?" Rhys asked.

"She's staying in for another night to get more fluids and rest," Claudia replied, careful not to share what the doctor had said. Just a few more days and her mother's prognosis might be much different. How had Karen not noticed?

"Does Mom know?"

"No. I'll tell her when your grandma is home and well again. There's no sense worrying her." That is what her mother had insisted on, and Karen should have the opportunity to enjoy her vacation.

Rhys nodded and went to the stove for another helping of spaghetti.

"Do you have homework?"

"No, just studying for exams. My first one is math, on Monday. Then I have three more the week after."

"And you're ready for math?"

"Of course." He scoffed.

"Then you and I have some decorating to do tonight," she said. "After we visit Grandma and shop for some groceries."

"Can Cam help?"

"Yes, if she's allowed to."

A prickly sensation crept up her spine, and she looked up to find Clint watching her. Their gazes locked, and she felt like prey caught in the sights of a hunter. She had to stop looking at him. The way he was watching her stirred up old feelings—feelings of longing. But longing for what, exactly?

"You haven't changed a bit, have you?" he said, a strange smile playing on his lips. "You always had everything under control." He turned to Rhys. "Your aunt here is the only reason I even graduated."

"I expect it was more because your mom wouldn't let you go out to see the world without your diploma," she said, trying to sound light, though the memories stung. She remembered the pain when he left. They'd talked so much of traveling the world together. When she had to stay to help her grandmother for a few months, she'd thought he would wait for her.

She'd been wrong.

Given the choice between staying with her and answering the call of adventure, adventure had won.

Clint had gone on without her, just as Alex seemed poised to do—right when she'd landed a good job in a career she loved.

"True," Clint said, drawing Claudia back to the conversation. "I've managed to see a lot of the world."

"But you finally settled… in Montreal, wasn't it?" she asked, taking another bite of spaghetti.

He held her gaze a beat longer than necessary before replying. "My wife settled there. The kids seem happy being near her family. But I never fit in."

"That can't be true," she said, though a part of her wondered how much of it was his own doing. Clint had a habit of rejecting others before they could reject him first.

"Her family doesn't think I'm good enough," he said, his voice tainted with bitterness. "They made things difficult. So I kept my distance. Since work took me all over the country, it was easy to stay away. We're separated now."

"But what about your kids?" asked Rhys, his voice cutting through the building tension.

"I see them for a few weeks at a time every two or three months. And we connect weekly over the internet since I moved out here."

"If it were me, I would miss my dad," Rhys said softly, and Claudia saw the memories of Adrian's illness flicker across his face. She wasn't the only one with memories that hurt.

Clint's smile faltered, a crack appearing in his tough exterior.

"That's why I'm considering a more permanent position on the mainland. To give them a place to visit me."

"You don't like it here?" asked Claudia. "There's a lot of building going on in this area."

"I do like it here," admitted Clint. "Spending time with Dad has been good, but I'm not sure this is where I want to settle. I need more—a bigger place, more to do."

Claudia nodded, understanding more than she wanted to. "The island does have its charms," she said, "but I get it." She hadn't felt like she belonged here for a long time. Ever since Karen moved back, she had felt superfluous. It was her sister's town now.

When Karen had returned to Sunshine Bay, married to a local boy, after getting her nursing degree, it only deepened Claudia's sense of not belonging. Claudia had left to get out from under her sister's shadow and to finally start her own life. To make her own mark on the world.

Yet now, when she was finally having success, it was like none of it mattered to Karen. Her sister could just call from the airport, expecting Claudia to drop everything, assuming her work wasn't important. Karen had a way of getting under her skin.

She pushed thoughts of her sister aside. "What would you do on the mainland?"

"Construction. Drywall."

"There is a lot going on over there," she said, knowing that was an understatement. Thousands of people were moving there every month, and they all needed houses, schools, hospitals, all manner of infrastructure.

"Yes, I'm counting on that," he said. "The company I work with has projects lined up. Once the building up at the college is done, I'll be moving."

She hesitated, her heart thudding louder than it should. Part of her wanted to say, "Look me up when you get there. We could have lunch." But how could she say that without it sounding like an invitation for something more?

Did she want it to be?

Her eyes dropped to her empty plate. She could feel his gaze again—burning into her like it always had, stirring up memories she had long buried. Memories of stolen kisses and whispered promises. Of the ache when he left.

The temptation to look at him, to let the past sweep her up, almost overwhelmed her. Almost.

She stood suddenly, her knee knocking into the table as she pushed her chair back, nearly tipping her water glass in the process.

"Thanks for bringing the tree," she said, too brightly. "We should probably head out to see Mom if we want time to decorate tonight. We can't have Project Vivian stalling before we get started."

"Right," he said, his knowing smile unnerving her more than it had when they were younger. Clint had always known what she was thinking. Back then, it had been endearing. Now it was just dangerous—this certainty that he still had a hold over her. That all he had to do was reach out and she would come to him.

Just like before.

He stood too, placing his plate on the counter. "I should go."

"Wait. I'll send some food home for your dad."

"Sure," he said, still watching her. His gaze followed her around the kitchen, heavy and intense, making her feel exposed. When she handed him the container, their hands brushed, and she nearly dropped it. How could this connection still be there after all these years? How could it burn after everything that had happened?

"Thanks," he murmured, his gaze flickering down to where their hands had touched, as if he felt it too.

"You're welcome," she said, wiping her hands on a tea towel. She needed to do something, anything, to break the spell. Then she followed him to the door and closed it firmly behind him. Leaning against it, she took a deep breath, her heart racing.

"You okay?" Rhys asked, stepping into the foyer, concern etched on his face.

"Of course," she said quickly, pushing herself away from the door. "Why do you ask?"

"No reason." He glanced at the door before turning back to her.

"I'm just going to put the dishwasher on, and then we can go. Okay?"

"What time do you think we'll be back?"

"Around eight, eight thirty?"

"Can Cam just come with us? She likes shopping. And I want Grandma to meet her."

"Sure," she said, turning away from the front door, eager to put distance between herself and any lingering memory of Clint.

CHAPTER 8

Vivian arrived home three days later and, with Claudia's assistance, dragged herself up the few steps to her porch. When she arrived at the top, winded as though she'd just climbed a mountain, she teetered a little and quickly grasped the railing.

"You okay, Mom?" asked Claudia, reaching out to steady her.

"I'm fine," Vivian snapped, brushing her daughter's hand away in irritation. At Claudia's shocked expression, she added, "I just need to catch my breath." But she was shaken. At no point had she ever thought of her front steps as Mount Everest, much less found each step so hard to navigate.

And it scared her. Especially since Karen had been on about her moving into a smaller, more manageable place to live. Now Claudia felt she had to help her with life's basics. Her daughters thought she was weak, feeble. Well, that was just too bad, because she was going to show them she was just fine. Starting now.

She let go of the railing and turned toward the door, where she caught a glimpse of her reflection in the window. The woman in the glass looked better than she had in a while. The nurses at the hospital had helped her bathe and do up her snow-white hair in a becoming style. She needed a trim, but a quick trip to the salon would remedy that. All in all, she looked damn good.

"Mom?"

"What?" She turned toward Claudia, who was examining her carefully.

"Do you need help?"

"Of course not," she said sharply, but she softened again at Claudia's expression. "Don't worry, I'm fine."

"Here, let me unlock the door. I have keys." Claudia's voice was gentle as though she were speaking to a child. Why did people speak to old people and children in the same way, as if they might break at any moment?

"Give them to me," she snapped again, and this time she didn't feel guilty. Offering help was one thing, but condescending to her outside her own home? That just burned her biscuits.

Claudia handed her the keys as if they, or maybe her mother, might bite her, and took a step out of the way. Then Vivian, despite her fluster at being watched as if she were a child who might make a mistake, found the key she needed quickly and put it in the lock. She pushed open the door to the scent of pine, stepped into the foyer, and nearly walked into Rhys. "Hey, Grandma! You're home. You look great!" He said as he swooped in to hug her.

"Did I ever tell you that you are my favorite grandson?" she asked.

"I'm your only grandson," he laughed. When he released her, she felt alone again, disconnected from the world, so she reached out to grasp his arm.

"Tell me what you have been up to since yesterday." She pulled every ounce of energy she could muster from her aching and bruised body to flash a smile she hoped seemed warm and genuine.

"Come and see." Rhys pulled her to the living room and swept his arm around in a flourish. Vivian's smile slipped.

"What's all this?" she asked, willing her teeth to unclench so she sounded curious rather than enraged. She could see perfectly well what it was.

Decorations. The decorations she had always hung with Ned. It was their tradition to pick out each one, sharing memories that each bauble brought to mind. The ones the kids made, the ones they had found while traveling together, gifts from people who were important to them. She didn't want these decorations up if he wasn't here to share those memories.

She wanted to run around the room, rip things down, and hide them away again, deep in the basement where she hadn't gone in months.

If Ned couldn't enjoy them, how could she?

But then she saw the hopeful look on Rhys's face and didn't have the heart to let her anger and despair bubble to the surface.

"Do you like it, Grandma?" he asked. "The tree is from our house, and Claudia and I found the box of decorations downstairs. Mom and Dad won't be decorating.

They're getting back only a few days before Christmas, and Mom is planning to come here."

"Here?" Vivian didn't want everyone here. She wanted to just sleep through the whole season and pretend it was still last November. What made Karen think it would be okay to just invite herself and her family anyway?

"We'll help," said Rhys. "Claudia promised to show me how to make a turkey dinner."

"Really?" Vivian's eyebrow lifted as she turned her gaze on her youngest daughter. "And when was the last time you made a turkey dinner?"

"I made one on Thanksgiving," said Claudia. "We had friends over, and I used the recipe you sent me, remember?"

Vivian tried to remember, but nothing came from the depths of her brain. "I'm glad the directions were clear," she said, covering up for her flagging memory. What was wrong with her? She had been struggling to remember basic things for months, but she didn't dare share that with her daughters or she would find herself on the list for an assisted care home within the hour.

She would rather die. She was only seventy-two, for heaven's sake.

Focus, she told herself. Going to a home wasn't something she was forced to do, and Karen, who was most likely to do the forcing, wasn't here anyway. Vivian had to keep her attention only on those who were in the room.

So she dug deep, calling forth the energy to visit with the daughter she rarely saw and a grandson who needed to be protected from her anguish so it didn't interfere with his studies.

And she had to do it soon, because they were both standing in the middle of the living room, watching her like she was a snake about to strike.

Or a woman about to collapse.

"The decorations look very nice, Rhys." He looked relieved, and she congratulated herself for doing the right thing. Then she turned to Claudia. "Thank you for coming to pick me up. I know you probably had to take time off work for that."

"Don't worry about it, Mom. You are more important than work. Would you like to lie down? Or maybe have a cup of tea?"

Lying down sounded like a great idea, but she had to force herself to stay up for a little while first. Try to be sociable. Ned would have been sociable if he were here.

"I would love a cup of tea," she said.

"Rhys, can you help your grandmother to the kitchen?" asked Claudia. "I'll put the kettle on."

"Come on, Grandma," he said putting his arm around her shoulders. She leaned into him a little.

"You must have grown a foot since the last time I saw you," she said.

He laughed. "I'll be as tall as Dad soon."

His father was six foot three, a great giant of a man who was a match for Helen, her five-foot-ten-inch daughter who had taken after her father's side of the family. Claudia, at five foot five, took after her.

She walked slowly into the kitchen, where Claudia bustled around, putting the teapot and cups onto a tray, finding the sugar and milk, Vivian had missed Claudia since she had moved to the mainland. And she had only been home once since her father's funeral, most likely at Alex's request.

She hoped Claudia would settle down with Alex. He was a nice man. Steady. Kind. A lot like Ned.

"How is Alex?" she asked when she'd sat in the chair closest to the door, having run out of energy to move much further.

"He's well," said Claudia. "His parents are at the apartment. Their flight out to see relatives was canceled because of the big snowstorm in Ontario."

"Helen is in that havoc as well, from what Tom has told me."

"Did Tom visit you, then?" Claudia asked, thwarting Vivian in her attempt to steer the conversation to her daughter's love life. She had to admire her daughter's skill at turning the conversation back to her.

"He feels bad that the dog was let out earlier last week," she said. "I told him to just keep the dog leashed from now on and things would go along well."

Rhys laughed. "Easier said than done."

"What do you mean?" asked Claudia, as she took the whistling kettle off the stove, poured a little water into the teapot, and rinsed it out before adding the tea leaves and letting it steam a moment. She was making tea the way Vivian had taught her years ago. Maybe the girl really would be able to cook a turkey dinner without much help. Vivian hoped so. She just didn't have it in her this year.

"That dog is an escape artist," said Rhys. "Cam saw him running way down near her place last week. Poor old Tom was having a hard time keeping up with him."

"Hopefully Joe and Helen will be home soon." Claudia poured in the boiled water, put on the lid, then put the Christmas-themed tea cozy onto the pot. Ned had found that cozy for her at a craft fair years earlier, and had given it to her as one of her twelve presents. She numbly watched Claudia set out teacups, milk and sugar, and spoons.

"Do you want something to eat?" Claudia sked. "I brought some nice tea buns from the bakery. And some cookies."

"Yes, please," said Rhys, sitting down at the chair across from Vivian.

"Not sure why I even asked," said Claudia. "This one is perpetually hungry."

Vivian smiled at the joke because she knew it was

expected, but she couldn't keep her eyes off the tea cozy. Yet another reminder that Ned was gone.

"Would you like one, Mom?"

Vivian looked up to find the buns and cookies on the table in front of her with butter and jam. When had that happened?

She shook her head, trying to focus on the present. "Sorry. I was woolgathering."

"It's okay. You must be tired. The doctor said you would be for a while."

"Yes," said Vivian. "That's it. Just tired."

"Well, let's get you to bed for some rest," said Claudia. "This afternoon I thought we could bake for the Community Tree Festival tomorrow."

"The festival is tomorrow?"

"Yes, and since it's been twenty-five years since you and Dad helped found it, we thought you might like to make a quick appearance. If not, I can go alone." But Claudia didn't look like she wanted to go alone.

Vivian tried hard to focus on Claudia, who seemed to be at the end of the gloomy tunnel Vivian had inhabited for nearly a year now. Her daughter was reaching out, urging her to reach back, and she couldn't let her down. She already owed her so much.

"Yes, of course I'll come," she found herself saying. "And I'll help with the baking." She and Claudia had baked together in the past, and it was always fun to share the work with someone who loved it as much as she did.

"Great!" said Rhys. "Our jazz quartet is playing at the festival. Can you come and watch me between eleven and twelve, or at two in the afternoon?"

"That's right," Claudia said. "I forgot you were in both bands. Is that why you've had so much practicing to do?"

"We have the big concert at the end of next week," said Rhys, "but the quartet is playing three times this weekend."

"I wouldn't miss it for the world," said Vivian, and a small sliver of light entered her tunnel world, courtesy of her grandson's huge smile.

"Your parents will be disappointed to miss it," said Claudia.

"They come to all my concerts, so it's okay if they miss these ones. Besides, a buddy of ours is filming it, so I can send them the recording."

"Technology is wonderful," said Vivian, forcing herself to stay in the conversation. "They'll really appreciate you sending it to them."

"Finish your tea, Mom. Then I'll help you to bed for a bit."

Vivian picked up the cup that Claudia must have set in front of her, and drained it of the cooling tea. "Yes. I think that will be best."

In a few minutes she was tucked under fresh sheets, with the blinds drawn so she was in darkness. She closed her eyes and dove into dreamland to find Ned again. And he was there, waiting for her.

Vivian awakened to yelling. She felt truly rested for the first time in a long time. She lay there a moment, trying to remember her dream, but her tentative memories vanished when the shouting came again from outside her bedroom window.

What was going on?

She stumbled to the window and drew up the blinds to look into the backyard, where a game of catch-the-dog was in progress.

Neville must have slipped from Tom's grasp again, and Rhys, Claudia, and Tom were attempting to corner the little guy. But they came up empty-handed whenever they lunged for his collar.

"Come on, Neville," said Rhys. "I'm going to be late for band practice if you don't come soon." He leaned forward to grasp at the dog's collar and ended up teetering over onto the grass.

"Ned, you would laugh at this," Vivian said, chuckling at the spectacle below. "Your grandson is so vexed right now. He's going to have to change before he can go out."

She provided the absent Ned with a play-by-play of Neville's antics until finally the dog made the mistake of running into a corner and the three of them descended upon him long enough for Rhys to catch him, and Tom to snap his leash onto his collar. The little dog didn't seem to mind. He just barked happily as though saying, "Fair play. You caught me." Though he was already wriggling loose again, intent on continuing the game.

Vivian laughed out loud at the dog's gumption, then went to the bathroom to have a shower. The warm water eased some of the soreness of her bruises, and when she emerged and toweled off, she felt much better. Then she moved around the room, getting dressed and doing her hair. She located a pair of slacks she hadn't worn in ages and a sweatshirt with a snowman print, appropriate for the season. When she slipped them on, she found they were bigger than they had been the year before, but when she looked in the mirror, she looked decent. If she added a little makeup, she might just be presentable.

When Claudia knocked on her door a while later, she called for her to come in.

"Oh good, you're already dressed! I was just coming in to see if you still wanted to get up and help me with the baking," said Claudia, stepping forward to give her a hug. "You're looking much better." Vivian hugged her back carefully. It felt good to hug. It was the thing she missed most about Ned. He had been an extraordinary hugger.

"Come and have a bit of soup," said Claudia. "I made beef barley. Then we can start. I'm looking forward to this. It's been a few years since I did much baking. I thought we could make sugar cookies and ice them like we used to."

"I always make a Battenberg cake as well," said Vivian. "I should probably continue the tradition. There's one lady who buys it every year, and I don't want to let her down."

"Oh, good. I've never made one, so you can teach me."

They ate a leisurely meal, and Vivian caught Claudia up on all the comings and goings of the people she had grown up with.

"How long has Clint been back?" Claudia asked casually, after they'd talked about who had children, who had moved away, who'd gotten married, and who'd gotten divorced.

Vivian's stomach clenched at the question. Guilt washed over her as she answered. "About eight months. He came back to town to work on an addition to the college, and I think to spend time with his father while he got his feet back on the ground."

"Feet back on the ground?"

"He's going through a divorce, from what I hear," said Vivian.

"I wondered about that when he told me he was separated, but didn't he get divorced years ago?"

"Oh, he did. This was his second marriage."

"Second? He's not even forty."

"Tom thinks he's still searching for something and trying to find it in marriage."

"Maybe he hasn't met the right woman yet," mused Claudia.

"Perhaps," said Vivian, carefully observing Claudia and hoping her daughter had gotten Clint out of her system years earlier. But it was clear there was more than a little interest there. When Clint had left town all those years before, and Claudia had stayed home to help with her grandmother, separating the two of them was the one thing about the situation that had *not* made Vivian feel guilty.

And then, when he found someone new so quickly, she felt Claudia had been fortunate. Neither of them had been old enough to get married—certainly not Clint, at any rate.

She and Claudia had tried to discuss Clint once before, not long after they'd learned he was staying in

Australia, but the conversation had only caused Claudia to break down in tears. They had never discussed him again. Until today.

"Are you finished? I think we should start baking or we'll be icing cookies at midnight," said Claudia.

"I'm ready." Vivian rose from her chair and went to the sink to rinse the bowls, put them in the dishwasher, and wash her hands. "We should try to get most of it done before my cleaner comes. I like to stay out of her way when she's washing floors and such."

"She's already been and gone."

"I never even heard her."

"You were exhausted. I'm glad you took the time to sleep."

They spent the afternoon and evening mixing batter, cutting out snowmen, bells, Santas, and holly leaves, preparing icing in several colors, piping on eyes and mouths, and stacking the cookies in the containers Vivian had been using for years. Just before six thirty, they were done everything but frosting the cake.

"I'll add the marmalade later tonight after it cools," said Vivian. "And I need to pick up some marzipan."

"Would you like something to eat?" asked Claudia. "I can buy you a light dinner while we're out getting marzipan."

"It would be good to get a salad or something light," said Vivian.

"I saw a little café near here when I was driving back from the hospital. Something to do with bees, I think."

"The Hive," said Vivian. "Yes, my friend Madge used to go there for lunch sometimes. I haven't been there in a long time, but it is pretty good."

Claudia drove Vivian to the café, where they settled into a booth in the cheerfully decorated room. Bees, honey, and sunflowers were the theme most of the year, but today the owners had added snow to the top of flowers and Santa hats to the bees. Santa and his sleigh hung from the ceiling, pulled by eight bees instead of reindeer.

"This is whimsical," said Claudia, laughing a little in delight, just as she had when she was a little girl. It was something Vivian had always appreciated about her daughter. No matter what life threw at her, she put a positive spin on things.

Usually.

When they had ordered and sat with their drinks waiting for their food, Vivian finally asked what she had been wanting to ask all week.

"Tell me, how are you and Alex doing?"

Claudia's face shuttered, and she shifted uncomfortably in her chair. "I don't know, Mom. We had a big fight the day I left to come here."

"I'm sorry I pulled you out of your life. I'm feeling much stronger now. You should go home and be with him. I don't want to get in your way." Especially since she felt Claudia had always blamed her when Clinton broke things off all those years ago.

"We had the fight before I talked to Karen. It was about him and his career and his needs. He's making decisions without even considering me and my needs."

"I'm sorry to hear that," said Vivian. She didn't want to pry, but she did want to know what had happened so she could help or at least offer a different perspective.

"He doesn't want to do the work he's been doing since we met. He wants to work in family law. And he applied for a job and wants to move away from Vancouver."

"Where is the job?"

"Victoria."

"His parents are getting older, and his siblings all live quite a way from here. Maybe he just wants to be near them so he can help them out if they need it."

Claudia looked at her with surprise. "I didn't think of that. "

"We took your father's mother in when she had her stroke," said Vivian, and then she immediately wished she had said nothing.

"Yes, I know. That was why Dad asked me to do my degree at the college here in town."

Now it was Vivian's turn to be surprised. "What do you mean your father asked you to stay?"

"He said that the family—you—needed help. Karen had a family of her own."

"Is that why you were always so angry with me?"

"I don't remember being angry." Claudia looked out the window, no longer looking her in the eye.

"I don't remember teaching you that it's okay to lie to

your mother," Vivian countered. "I didn't know your father asked you to stay."

"He said that it would only be for a few months, or a year at most. I could do my first year of college here and then join Clint on his travels when he got to Europe. But then, well, you know."

"Clint married another woman."

She nodded. "Then Grandma had her second stroke, so I decided to finish my second year here, and then my third. It just got harder and harder to leave."

"But you did leave," said Vivian. "And you got a master's degree. A good job. And Alex seems nice."

"But now he wants to leave Vancouver, and I feel like I have to choose between him and my career. My friends are there now."

"You can always make more friends."

"But it's so hard. Why does life have to be so hard, Mom?"

"I wish I knew," said Vivian. "This year has been the hardest year of my life. I keep wishing I could wake up and it would be back to normal. But there is no normal, is there? Only change." Tears crowded her eyes, and she fought them back. No wonder she was dehydrated. She kept crying all the time, even after all these months.

"I'm sorry, Mom. I didn't mean to burden you. You have enough to worry about without my stuff."

"My grandmother used to say a problem shared is a problem halved. Though some problems are harder than others. Have you spoken to Alex about how you feel?"

"A bit. We'll talk more when he gets here. I'm just not sure what I want. And now…"

"Now?"

"Nothing." Claudia shook her head. "We should get that marzipan and get home."

Vivian narrowed her eyes on her daughter, wondering what was going on in that head of hers. Alex was a man who put family first. He even visited Vivian when he came to the island to see his own parents, though they never told Claudia about those visits, nor about the chores he did for her around the house, like changing lightbulbs and helping with her computer access.

Both Claudia and Karen were busy women, dealing with their own grief over losing their father. Vivian didn't want to be a burden, but Alex seemed to enjoy the visits as much as she did. He liked to feel useful and see a project finished, he'd told her one day. And Ned had elicited a promise that if anything should ever happen to him, Alex would help where he could.

"Did he tell you he was sick?" Vivian asked Alex on one of his visits.

"No. We had all had a bit to drink—me and Blaine and Ned. We had gone out to the pub to shoot some pool the day after Boxing Day. When we came back to the house, Ned asked Blaine and me to promise that if anything should happen to him, we would help you out. I thought it was because Blaine's father-in-law had passed the year before, and because Ned was in his seventies, feeling like he had more time behind him than in front of him. I didn't know he was sick."

"I should have said something earlier. Claudia is so hurt that I waited so long to call and tell her to come. But he didn't want her or Blaine to see him that way, I suppose because neither of them was in the medical field. Karen was more used to it. She worked in hospice for a few years."

"Still, if it's okay with you, I won't mention to Claudia that I come and help. At least not right now. Can we

keep it between us? She might think I knew more and kept it from her. She'd never forgive me for that."

"You don't need to come. It's a long way," Vivian said.

"I gave Ned my word. And I consider you family. You and Ned helped us when we needed it," he said. "If it hadn't been for the down payment you gave us to put on the condo, we never would have been able to buy in this market. It has set us up for success."

"That was Claudia's inheritance. From her grandmother."

"It may have been earmarked for her, but it was left to you. I don't want you to think we don't appreciate it. Besides, even if you hadn't been able to help us, I would come just for a piece of this Battenberg cake," he said, taking a bite of the cake on the plate. "This is seriously fantastic."

She had laughed at him and agreed not to tell Claudia about the visits. Alex thought Claudia hadn't come because of her grief over her father, but Vivian knew differently. Claudia was afraid—afraid that if she visited, she would be sucked into caring for her aging mother. Just like she'd been forced to look after her grandmother when Vivian couldn't cope.

Well, if Claudia thought her mother couldn't cope this time, she would prove her wrong. She levered herself out of the chair and congratulated herself that she didn't teeter as she had the day before. She was getting stronger every day, and if Claudia was reconsidering her relationship with Alex, it would not be down to her mother. Claudia would need to make that decision for herself.

CHAPTER 9

*W*hen they arrived at the festival the following morning, Rhys climbed out of the car first, grabbed his saxophone, and hurried to join his bandmates.

"Shall we find a table to sit and have tea?" asked Claudia, after they handed over their cookies and cake to the baking table. The woman taking them was suitably impressed by the work involved, and exclaimed that Mrs. Wimple, the woman who always came for the cake, would be ecstatic. "She loves your Battenberg cake, Vivian. Says that it's just like the one her mother used to make when she was a little girl back in England."

"Happy to help," said Vivian, and Claudia was pleased to see her mother's cheeks turn pink from the unexpected praise. Her mom looked more herself today. Maybe Tom Jones was right, and all her mother needed was to find something to contribute to and spend more time with people.

She would make time to visit him in the next few days to give him an update and ask if he had any more ideas. The festival was a good one.

"What would you like to do first?" she asked, once they had left the bake sale.

"Let's take a walk around and see what people have done this year," said Vivian. "I like to look at the Christmas trees."

Each of the trees had been decorated and donated by a local business. Tickets were on sale to raffle them off, and all proceeds went to charity. This year there were several entries from artisans and others.

"Look at this one," said Claudia, when they got to the yarn shop's entry. "All the little ornaments that look like penguins and bears. Didn't you used to knit things like this, Mom?"

Vivian smiled at the memory. "Yes, I used to do a lot of knitting, though I believe these are crocheted."

"Right," said Claudia, acknowledging the correction.

"I even belonged to a knitting guild until a few years ago."

"Why did you stop?"

"I don't know. I guess after Marge died, I didn't have anyone to go with."

"Tom's wife?" Claudia asked, reaching up to touch one of the little cats that seemed remarkably lifelike.

"We used to carpool, and we'd plan our next projects together, and I just found it hard after she died. I missed her so much. Besides, your father wanted me to spend more time with him after he retired completely. So I guess I gave it up."

"Would you like to try it again?" asked Claudia.

"Maybe. I have a few projects in my closet that I haven't finished."

"We should dig them out tomorrow," said Claudia. "Could you show me how to make these?" She pointed at a pair of polar bears sporting red scarves.

"You want to learn to crochet?"

"Yes," said Claudia, though she was only saying so to get her mother back into the habit. "I should find something to do in the evenings when it's cold. This looks like fun."

"Well, then, let's do that," said Vivian. "It'll give us something to do together."

"I'd like that," said Claudia, knowing this at least was true. Baking cookies and learning to make a Battenberg cake had been fun, and it pulled on her creative side more than anything she had done since her art classes in high school.

"They're selling the patterns for these over there." Vivian pointed to a neighboring booth. "Let's see how hard it is and whether I have the materials already."

Vivian made a beeline to the booth for Stitching Dreams, the local fabric and yarn shop, and flashed a huge smile. "Gemma, how are you?"

"Vivian!" said Gemma, a forty-something woman who was busy rearranging her booth after what appeared to be a stock clear-out. Claudia hoped she still had the pattern for the bears. "It's been ages!"

"I'd like you to meet my daughter Claudia," said Vivian. "We're after that pattern for the amigurumi bears on your tree."

"Oh, I have a copy of the book," said Gemma. "Let me grab it." She bent to look under the table and popped up with the book.

Vivian perused it and said, "This will be perfect. I have enough wool and the right hooks at home to start."

She handed it over to Claudia. "Look and see if it's what you want, dear."

As Claudia leafed through the pages of patterns, she watched her now-animated mother catching up with Gemma, asking her how business was doing and about her children. Other than the weight loss and slightly drawn face, her mother looked just as Claudia remembered. Even better than she had the previous Christmas.

But she was still missing her usual sparkle, which reminded Claudia she would have to talk her mother into seeing the doctor. Grief, like her mother's, was normal, but there was a fine line between grief and deep depression. Claudia was afraid her mother may have crossed that line.

.   .   .

*a*nother woman Claudia didn't know greeted her mother and talked her into going off to see a mutual friend, who was sitting nearby having a cup of coffee.

"Go ahead," said Claudia. "I'll just get this"—she pointed to the book—"and look around for a bit."

Her mother nodded at her, distracted by the conversation. She was soon heading toward the tables.

Claudia was handing the book and her credit card to Gemma when she heard a familiar voice behind her.

"I didn't know you crocheted."

She turned to see Clint, his lazy, sexy smile lighting up his face as he looked down at her.

"I don't yet," she replied, taking back her card and slipping it into her purse. "Mom used to knit, and I thought if she taught me, it might spark her interest again. Part of my Project Vivian efforts."

"Your mother is a brilliant teacher," Gemma chimed in, interrupting their conversation. "She used to help a lot of women in the guild. I wish I had her on my staff."

Claudia laughed softly. "Are you hiring? It might be nice for her to have something like this to do once or twice a week."

Gemma's eyes lit up. "I'm always looking for workshop leaders. Do you think she'd be interested? I haven't seen much of her these past few years."

"I could ask," Claudia said. "She lost Dad earlier this year, and it might help to have something new to focus on."

"We were all so sorry to hear about Ned," Gemma said, her tone sympathetic. "He was such an asset to our town. Everyone loved him."

"Yes, I know," Claudia whispered, her throat tightening. "We all miss him." She took a deep breath. "But I'm now focusing on helping Mom figure out what she wants to do next. It's been a hard year for her, and I want her to find something to look forward to. Though she seems happy today."

"She's always been so good with people. It's wonderful to see her out again." Gemma handed Claudia the book. "Good luck with the bears," she said with a smile.

"Thanks," Claudia replied. "I'll probably need it. Mom's the one with all the skills."

"Well, you have the best teacher."

Claudia nodded goodbye and turned back to Clint, who had been waiting patiently, his gaze lingering on her.

"I didn't think Christmas tree festivals were your thing," she teased, hoping to lighten the tension forming between them.

Clint grinned. "Dad wanted to make sure everything was set up properly. He's part of the group that organizes the trees and tables every year. He's also selling raffle tickets." Clint gestured to a table where his father, Tom, was deep in conversation with another man. As they walked over, Claudia noticed that Tom's expression tightened slightly when he saw Clint, though he smiled warmly at her.

How odd, Claudia mused. Was there something going on between Clint and his father?

"Hello, Claudia," Tom said warmly. "Did your mother come too?"

"She's over there, catching up with some old friends," Claudia said, gesturing toward a group of women whose laughter was filling the room. "I'm here to buy some raffle tickets."

Tom smiled as he looked in the direction of her mother. "It's good to see her out again. She looks happy." Then he turned back to Claudia. "How many tickets can I get you? One? Three? Ten?"

"Let's go with ten," she said, handing him a ten-dollar bill.

As Tom handed her the tickets, Claudia felt Clint's eyes on her. She couldn't help but glance at him—and notice the way his jaw tightened as Tom turned away. There was a subtle undercurrent she couldn't quite put her finger on.

As she filled out her tickets, she glanced at Clint, who seemed content to watch her. She placed her tickets in the boxes for the trees she liked best: the one adorned with hand-blown glass ornaments, another with wood cutouts, and the third with the crocheted figures she had admired earlier.

"Gambling is a bad habit," Clint teased, his voice light but his gaze intense.

"This isn't gambling," she said, grinning up at him, though the air between them felt charged. "It's supporting a good cause while having a little fun."

"You could just vote with a token, you know."

"I know," Claudia said, "but this way, I get to support something meaningful."

"I suppose," Clint said, following her as they moved back toward her mother.

"Do you want a coffee?" he asked suddenly, his voice lowering.

"I was thinking of getting tea," she said. "Too much coffee makes me jittery."

"Have a seat," he said. "I'll get it for you. What do you take?"

"Just milk," she said, glancing over at the table where her mother was surrounded by friends and clearly enjoying herself.

She found an empty table nearby, her thoughts racing as she sat down. The tension between them lingered in her mind, unsettling her more than she cared to admit.

As Clint got their drinks, Claudia watched the room. Children were scattered around, getting their faces painted, listening to a story, and watching a clown make them each a balloon animal. On the stage, Rhys and his band were setting up. Soon, the sound of Christmas music filled the room, and Claudia found herself lost in the melody.

"Here you go," Clint said, returning with her tea. "Just milk."

"Thank you," she said, taking the cup from him.

"Is that Rhys?" he said, sitting beside her.

"Yes," Claudia said, smiling. "He's been practicing a lot, and it shows. They sound great."

"You used to play in the band. Do you still play?" Clint asked.

"I played the clarinet only until we graduated. Though, listening to him, I'd take up the saxophone now if I didn't think I'd embarrass myself."

"I'm sure you could if you wanted to. You were always good at everything you did," Clint said, his voice low, intimate.

Claudia swallowed, feeling the weight of his words. "Thank you," she said, trying to turn her attention to the music instead of the intensity in Clint's gaze. His eyes had once had the ability to convince her to do anything —except, she supposed, follow him to Australia.

What if I had gone with him? she wondered for a fleeting moment, then decided to charge ahead and ask.

"So how have you been?" she asked. "It's been ages since you left for Australia."

"I've been…okay," Clint said, taking a sip of his coffee. "I worked at a bar there for a few years, then drifted a bit. I liked it until I didn't."

"What made you change your mind?"

"I met a girl," Clint said, his voice growing quieter. "Her family didn't approve of me. So I left her…and my daughter. She's almost nineteen now."

Claudia's heart ached as she processed the words. "I'm sorry, Clint."

"It was my fault," he said. "I was angry. Angry that you didn't come with me. Angry at myself for some bad choices I made. And I moved on too quickly."

"I told you I'd come after I finished my semester," Claudia said, her eyes locking with his.

He shook his head. "You weren't coming, Claudia. We both knew that."

She blinked in surprise. "I was. At least I thought I was. When I heard you were getting married six months after you left, it broke my heart."

Clint looked away, his jaw tightening. "Your dad told me you weren't coming. He warned me off."

"My dad did that?"

"He told me you'd never leave. And when you stayed to take care of your grandmother, I figured he was right."

Claudia's chest tightened. "I promised him I'd finish my semester, but after that... I *was* going to come, Clint. Then I heard you were getting married."

"Who told you?"

"Your sister. I ran into her when she was visiting your dad for Christmas. I went to ask for your new address because my emails bounced."

Clint's face went pale. "You mean...you were planning to come?"

"Yes," she said softly. "I was saving up, working, and I was ready. But by then, you had started your new life without me."

Clint searched her eyes, his face filled with regret. "I didn't know. I would've waited if I'd known."

She sighed, the weight of the past pressing down on her. "It doesn't matter now. We've both moved on."

"I guess we have," he said, though he didn't sound convinced. "But I wonder sometimes what would've happened if you'd come with me."

"I used to wonder too," she admitted, before she could stop herself.

"Are you in a relationship now?" he asked, his eyes searching hers.

"I've been with Alex for six years," she said, her voice quiet.

"And how's that going?" he asked. His tone was casual, but the question hit too close to home.

Claudia hesitated, looking around the room as the band wrapped up their set. "We're at a crossroads," she finally said.

"What kind of crossroads?" Clint leaned in, his curiosity piqued.

"He wants to move," she said, feeling a pang of frustration. "Just when I've landed my dream job."

"And you've put your career first all this time," Clint said, his voice understanding.

"Yes," Claudia said quietly. "I've worked so hard to get where I am, and now he wants to start fresh somewhere else. Raise kids."

"And you're not ready to give that up?" Clint asked.

"No," she said, surprised by how certain she felt. "I've waited a long time to get here."

Clint nodded slowly. "You've always been driven. It's one of the things I admire about you."

She smiled, appreciating his words. "I just don't know what to do. I thought Alex was the one, but I'm not sure we have the same dreams anymore."

Clint's gaze softened. "You've built something, and you don't have to give that up. Maybe he'll understand if you're honest with him. Maybe you can find a compromise."

Claudia sighed. "I hope you're right."

"If you were my partner, I would certainly try. You're worth it."

Claudia's breath caught. She stared at him, feeling a sudden pull between them—old feelings mixing with new ones, confusing her even more.

"I need to go," she said suddenly, rising from her seat. The past was colliding too much with her present.

"Claudia," Clint started, reaching out as if to stop her, but she shook her head.

"I'll see you around." She grabbed her coat and walked out of the tension-filled hall, unsure of what she felt and even less certain of what she wanted.

She was almost outside when she heard her mother. "Claudia, wait for me."

When she turned she saw her mother rushing toward her. "I'm glad you're ready to go," Vivian said, slowing down as she approached. "I'm getting tired, and Rhys is going to get a ride home with Cam's father."

"I was just stepping outside for some fresh air," said Claudia. "I would have been back for you soon."

"Well, now there is no need." Her mother smiled brightly.

They stepped out into the crisp, cold air, and her mother turned to her, a knowing look on her face. "I saw you talking to Clint. You two still have unfinished business, don't you?"

Claudia blinked in surprise. "What do you mean?"

Her mother smiled sadly. "I mean I don't think you ever really let him go."

Claudia opened her mouth to protest, but the words caught in her throat. She wasn't sure how to answer that —was it true? Had she been holding on all these years without even realizing it?

"Mom…" she started, but her mother waved her off.

"Don't worry. I'm not saying you have to do anything about it. Just know that sometimes those things we don't resolve have a way of coming back into our lives when we least expect it."

Claudia thought about Clint's eyes, the regret in his voice when he talked about their past, and the way her heart had skipped a beat when he asked if she was happy with Alex.

Maybe her mother was right. Maybe there was something she still needed to figure out—something she hadn't faced yet.

But for now, as they walked to the car, Claudia pushed her thoughts to the back of her mind. She could think about it later.

CHAPTER 10

*V*ivian woke smiling and ready to get going. She was looking forward to seeing more of her friends today.

The night before, after taking a rest and watching one of their favorite Christmas movies together, she and Claudia and Rhys had sat again at the kitchen table, making the four dozen rum balls she promised those running the baking table.

As the trio worked, they shared memories of Christmases past, particularly stories of Ned, how much he loved the season, and the lengths he would go to decorate the yard, bring people together, and show up as Santa all over town.

They shared stories, laughing until the tears came, but for the first time in a year, those tears were happy ones. And, for the second time in that year, she slept deeply.

When she got to the kitchen, Vivian found Rhys alone at the table, staring into his oatmeal.

"What's wrong? Did you lose something?"

"Huh?"

"You look like you're searching for something in your porridge."

"Maybe an answer."

"What's the question?" she asked, pouring herself a cup of coffee from the pot Claudia must have made that morning. She slipped into the chair across from him.

Rhys sighed, looked down at his oatmeal again, then searched the hallway behind Vivian before he met her eyes.

"I'm trying to decide if I should tell someone I like that they're maybe losing their girlfriend," he whispered.

Vivian raised an eyebrow. "Hmm. And your friend hasn't noticed?"

"Shhh." He leaned forward. "He's, um… out of town. She's here. So is her old boyfriend. And… Well, I like my friend a lot, and he doesn't even know what's going on."

Vivian took a sip of her coffee and whispered back. "Are we talking about someone I know?"

Rhys hesitated, looked furtively at the doorway again, then said, "Claudia. I think she's starting to have feelings for Clint."

Vivian leaned back. "What makes you think that?" she asked. "She was in the shower when I came down, by the way."

He seemed to relax a bit, knowing his aunt was likely out of earshot, but he still whispered. "The way they look at each other. She blushes, twirls her hair, and he looks like he's about to grab her and kiss her. And Alex is a nice guy." He frowned. "Clint seems nice enough, but he's still married, with kids he hardly sees. Cam thinks he's got issues. I just think if Alex were here, he could stop her from making a big mistake."

"He's coming for Christmas."

"That might be too late."

"This is Claudia's decision, Rhys."

"But what if someone were to tell Alex? At least give him a chance."

Vivian thought for a moment. "The most someone could do is suggest he visit early. Maybe to see the Lights on the Harbor Sailpast."

Rhys's face lit up. "Grandma, that's a great idea! I'll text him right now."

"Do you even have his number?"

"Of course! He's my uncle."

Rhys quickly finished his cereal, rinsed his bowl, and placed it in the dishwasher. "See you, Grandma!" he called as he rushed down the hall.

Vivian chuckled, but her amusement faded as she thought about what Rhys had said. This could end in disaster. Hopefully, Alex would give them a heads-up before he arrived.

If only Clint would go back to Quebec. Or better yet, Australia.

"Where is Rhys off to in such a hurry?" asked Claudia, stepping into the room with a cardboard box.

"Getting ready for the concert," said Vivian, knowing it was only a partial lie.

"We should get going soon too," said Claudia. "Have you eaten?"

"I was just going to have a piece of toast," said Vivian, getting up to pull some bread out of the freezer. Do you want some?"

"I had porridge," said Claudia setting the box on the counter and loading the bags of rum balls they had assembled the night before while she hummed "Jingle Bells."

"You seem happy," said Vivian.

"I am," said Claudia. "I had fun yesterday, and I'm hoping today will be just as good."

"I hope so too," said Vivian. "I'm looking forward to hearing Rhys and his band play again. Let me call Tom. I told him we would give him a ride this morning."

Twenty minutes later, Claudia drove them all to the festival, and when one of the volunteers called in sick, she offered to step up and help run the food counter.

So when Tom finished his shift at the raffle booth, he

and Vivian grabbed cups of hot cocoa and sat down to listen to the band and wait for Claudia to finish.

"It's good to see you out, Viv," Tom said.

"Thanks for reminding Claudia about the baking. She told me it was your suggestion to ask me to help. These last couple of days have felt almost normal—and after the year I've had, normal has been a blessing."

"Be patient, Viv. Grief takes the time it takes."

"I know, but after a year, people expect you to be past it. I just miss him so much," she said, her eyes beginning to water.

"I know you do." Tom reached across the table and patted her arm. "I miss him too. He was a good friend. If it weren't for Ned, I don't know where I'd be. Especially since Madge passed."

Vivian sighed. "How did you get over Madge's death?"

"Oh, I haven't. And I doubt I ever will. I don't really want to, to be honest."

"You seem happy when I see you."

"I'm not sad, though there are days when I miss her terribly. But she's still with me. She is part of who I am because, without her in my life, I would have been a very different person."

"You mean her spirit is still here?"

"Not in the way people think. Or at least not for me. For the first year, I held on to her, refused to believe she was gone. I expected to see her everywhere I turned. I even spoke to her. But then I had to stop doing that and let her go."

"I don't want to let Ned go," Vivian whispered.

"Maybe 'letting go' isn't the right phrase," Tom said thoughtfully. "It's more like… I keep going, but with her alongside me. She'll always be with me, always be a part of my life. But she can't be a part of my days the same way anymore. I needed to find other people, other purposes, to keep me moving forward."

"Isn't it lonely?"

"Sure, sometimes. But I have my kids, my friends. Even Neville keeps me company these days."

Vivian chuckled. "That dog. I can't believe I tripped over him."

"Well, on the upside, he got you out of the house for a while," Tom joked.

"You know, you're right. And he brought Claudia home. She hasn't been here much this year, and I've missed her. I think I've seen more of her boyfriend Alex than I have of her. She's still upset that I waited too long to tell her that her dad was sick. She almost didn't get to say goodbye."

Tears threatened again, and Tom reached over to squeeze her arm. "But he waited for her. Besides, she may not be coming home because when she does, it really hits home that he's gone. When she's in Vancouver, she can probably pretend that he's still just a phone call away. "

"I hadn't thought about it that way."

"You can't change the past, Viv. You just have to keep moving forward and try to enjoy the days you have left. That's all anyone can do."

Vivian glanced over at Claudia, who was serving a customer. "How's Clint doing?"

"I worry about him. This marital separation has been tough on him. I know he misses his kids, and I think he misses Yvette."

"I thought he and Yvette were happy. What happened?"

"Not sure. She says he hasn't ever fully committed to her. And maybe she's right. When I saw him here yesterday, I thought maybe he's still carrying a torch for your Claudia."

Vivian sighed. "Yes, I think you're right. And she hasn't let him go either."

"Yvette was good for him, and I think she still loves him. I've asked her to visit and bring the kids for Christmas."

"Do you think she'll come?"

"She told me she would let me know in the next couple of days. She needs to take time off work and get tickets, which will be hard at the last minute."

"What does Clint think? Is he looking forward to their visit?"

"I'm waiting until I hear from her before I tell him. I wanted it to be a surprise."

"Tom, I think you should tell him. Surprises like that can backfire, and at this time of year, you don't need to add any extra stress."

"You wouldn't wait?"

"No. He may be able to help with the tickets. And it would give him time to plan things. He'll want to be part of it."

"And if she decides not to come?"

"Then at least you tried."

"Okay. That's good advice. Thank you. But enough about that. What do have you planned for the next week? Now that you're out and about, you need to keep the momentum going."

"Tomorrow, I have two tasks, thanks to my family. After his test, I am to teach my grandson how to make a steak dinner. And after dinner, Claudia wants me to teach her how to crochet. Tuesday, I have a lunch planned with Helen, as long as she gets back in town tomorrow, and we are going to do some last-minute shopping. And Wednesday, another cooking lesson. Rhys wants to be able to make his parents dinner when they get back from Mexico."

"That's a great start."

"This Saturday is the sailpast. I offered to take Helen's place on the cocoa brigade and help serve the hot chocolate that evening."

"If they need any more help, let me know. I can lend a hand."

"I will. Now listen. It's time for Rhys's solo."

They turned their attention to the stage and Vivian smiled, appreciating every note. Today was a good day, she decided. And that was all she could ask for. One good day at a time.

CHAPTER 11

The week leading up to the Lights on the Harbor Sailpast flew by for Claudia. Between work, crochet lessons, and helping Rhys master the art of cooking, her time was completely consumed. She barely had a moment to think about anything else, though she did make sure to let Karen know that Rhys and their mother were doing fine. She also texted Alex every night, sharing pictures of her crochet attempts and small updates about what was happening.

He responded by sharing what was happening with his own week, just as they usually did when one of them was away, just like nothing had changed between them.

But change was coming, and she was going to have to decide what to do about it.

On Thursday evening, she finally found a chance to head downtown for some shopping. Even though her family had long ago agreed not to buy too many things no one would use past January, she still wanted to get experience-based gifts. She picked up season tickets to the theater for Karen and Adrian, cinema passes for Rhys, and an introductory pottery class for her mother.

Taking a break, Claudia stopped at a cozy coffee shop. She was surprised to spot Clint sitting alone, nursing a fresh cup of coffee.

She paused, her heart skipping a little faster. "Hello, stranger," she greeted him with a smile. "Mind if I join you?"

Clint looked up; his expression darkened by a deep scowl. "Sure," he muttered.

"What's wrong?" she asked, sliding into the seat across from him.

"My father's been up to mischief," he said, shaking his head. "He invited my wife and kids to come here for Christmas."

Claudia raised her eyebrows. "Don't tell me—your ex said no."

"No," Clint sighed, his frustration palpable. "Yvette said yes."

Her breath caught. "Then what's the problem?"

Clint's face tightened. "What if I mess it up and she never lets them visit again? Her family will hate the idea."

Claudia leaned in, her tone gentle but firm. "Clint, what do you want to happen? Sounds like you're putting up roadblocks before they even get here."

He rubbed his temples, clearly frustrated. "I don't know."

"Don't you?"

He stared down at the table and mumbled, "I want them back, Claudia."

"I see," said Claudia. Her heart sank, the realization hitting her hard. Whatever wisp of hope she had for rekindling their relationship vanished. How could she compete with the family he clearly still longed for?

"Have you told Yvette that?" she asked gently.

He hesitated. "No."

"Well, maybe you should. And tell her your plans for getting that permanent position."

"I haven't been planning that."

"When we talked last week, you said you were moving to Vancouver. To a more permanent position."

"I am. But Yvette would never want to move here. She wants to stay in Montreal where her family is."

"Have you asked her if she would consider coming here?"

His silence was all the answer she needed.

Claudia sighed, her own emotions churning. There was relief that she wouldn't have to face the temptation of starting something with Clint, but disappointment that he never really wanted her. She shook her head, keeping her voice steady. "Start with that, Clint. Ask her."

He nodded, as if coming to the realization himself. "Yeah… maybe."

Claudia blew out a breath, and a weight lifted. She couldn't help but feel rejected, but she knew now that Clint's future was with his family, not with her.

"I thought I knew what I wanted," Clint continued, "but being away from them so long has made me realize what I'm missing. I keep thinking about what Rhys said the other day when I told him I rarely saw them. He was horrified."

Claudia hesitated. "What happened between you? You don't have to answer if it's too personal."

Clint's voice softened. "I'm not even sure anymore."

"How did you meet?"

Clint smiled faintly, lost in the memory. "After I left Australia, I bummed around Europe for a couple of years. I met Yvette in France while she was visiting relatives. She's from Montreal. We hit it off and came back to Canada. Got married fifteen years ago, and then we had the kids."

Claudia thought about how different their lives were. Fifteen years. His life had been so different from hers.

"So... what do you think went wrong?"

Clint sighed. "Yvette got tired of me being away. She said she may as well be on her own since I was always working on projects around the country. Our life became empty. So now I've got two failed marriages and a lot of stamps on my passport."

"Sounds like you want things to be different now," Claudia said, though to her the answer was clear.

"Yeah. Something that lets me be with my kids more. And…"

"And?"

"I miss her. She was my best friend."

Claudia understood that feeling of losing your best friend. That was how she felt about Alex. She was losing him, but she worried that if she took steps to keep him, she would lose a part of herself.

They sat together, sipping coffee, and she listened to his plans, making a few suggestions, asking questions to help him think through the details.

And, as she listened, she realized she no longer felt a need to explore a relationship with Clint. His hold on her was gone.

She had let him go.

But now she had two decisions to make. Did she want to stay with Alex? And, if so, what did that mean for her career?

CHAPTER 12

*O*n the morning of December fourteenth, the day of the sailpast, Vivian woke late and crept into the kitchen, careful not to wake Rhys or bother Claudia. Her daughter was hard at work, catching up on what she had missed the previous week. She hoped Claudia didn't always work that hard. Years of being a nurse had taught her one important lesson: no matter how much you give to your job, your employer doesn't love you back.

Love came from family, friends, even neighbors—but never from work.

Vivian brewed herself a cup of tea and padded into the living room. She hadn't sat in Ned's old reclining chair for days, but today she needed the comfort. Easing back into the worn leather, she pressed the button to raise her feet and sighed. It felt good to relax after a week of activity.

As she lifted her cup to her lips, something outside caught her eye. She froze, her teacup clattering back onto the table. "Claudia! Rhys!"

"What's wrong?" Rhys burst into the room, eyes wide with alarm, and Claudia was hard on his heels.

"Look!" Vivian pointed out the window, her hand trembling. "The tree!"

Claudia squinted toward the tree, shading her eyes against the stream of morning sunlight. "It looks like… some kind of bird?"

"Rhys, get your grandfather's binoculars from the study, top shelf!" Vivian urged, fumbling with the recliner button, trying to get her feet down. Rhys stood there, still groggy, trying to make sense of what his grandmother was saying.

"Go!" Vivian snapped, her frustration bubbling over.

"I'll go," Claudia muttered, rolling her eyes. "Rhys, stay with your grandmother. Mom, calm down and have some tea. I'll be back in a second."

Vivian finally managed to lower her legs and rushed to the window, pressing her hands against the glass, her heart pounding. "Who would do this?" she murmured.

Moments later, Claudia returned with the binoculars. Vivian grabbed them with trembling hands. She adjusted the focus and gasped. "It's… an ornament. A bird, but there's something else…"

"What is it?" Claudia asked, leaning in.

"A number one. Hanging below the bird. A partridge in a pear tree," Vivian whispered, her voice thick with emotion.

Claudia took the binoculars from her mother. "It's definitely a Christmas ornament. But who would do this?"

"Someone with a strange sense of humor," Vivian grumbled.

"Or someone who wanted to give you a gift," said Rhys. "It is the fourteenth, after all. Counting today, there are twelve days until Christmas."

Vivian narrowed her eyes at Rhys. "Was it you?"

"No." Rhys held up his hands, clearly startled by the accusation. "It wasn't me."

Claudia chuckled, shaking her head. "Don't look at me, either. But whoever it is, they probably meant well."

"It just makes me miss him more," Vivian said, her voice cracking. She turned away from the window, eyes clouding over at the memories of Ned.

Claudia put a hand on her shoulder. "I know, Mom. But whoever did this... they care about you."

"Maybe it was Tom," Vivian said after a pause. "He's always doing little things like this for people."

Claudia smiled. "It does sound like something he would do."

"Well, it is pretty," Vivian admitted, picking up the binoculars again. "Made of metal, maybe tin? Does the 'one' mean there's more coming? Two turtle doves next?" She let out a shaky laugh. It felt bittersweet. The gesture wasn't from Ned, but someone out there still cared enough to keep the tradition alive for one more year.

As her excitement simmered down, Vivian sank back into the recliner, cradling her tea in her hands. *Whoever did this*, she thought, *I hope they know how much it means*. The mystery settled in her heart and, with it, a sense of quiet anticipation.

CHAPTER 13

*a*t four o'clock there was a knock at the door, and Claudia heard Vivian call from the kitchen. "Can you get that? I've got my hands full of biscuit dough."

Claudia opened the door and froze, her heart jumping in her chest.

"Alex," she whispered, blinking as if unsure he was real. "What are you doing here?"

"Rhys told me his band was playing tonight at the sail-past," Alex said, smiling sheepishly. "Figured I'd come by and finally hear them play."

"You didn't have to…" Her protest trailed off as Alex stepped forward, closing the space between them. He kissed her, and she surprised herself by kissing him back, enjoying the warmth of his embrace.

"I didn't have to, but I wanted to," he murmured against her lips. "Plus, I was checking on Mom and Dad's place, so I was kind of in the neighborhood."

She flushed as she pulled away, still flustered by his sudden appearance.

"I wasn't expecting you until next week. And, for the record, Victoria is nowhere near this neighborhood."

"I'm only here for tonight," he said, stepping inside as Claudia's mother called out from the kitchen, "but starting next week, I'll be here for the rest of the year. I'm off until after New Year's Day."

"Don't let the boy stand on the doorstep!" Vivian said again, coming in from the kitchen. "Come in, Alex."

Alex grinned and stepped inside, pulling off his boots. "Hey, Vivian. Claudia says you've been baking?" He sniffed the air hopefully.

She laughed. "I have, but no Battenberg cake this week."

Claudia's brow furrowed. "Wait. When did you ever have Mom's Battenberg cake?"

"Last Christmas," Alex said, a teasing glint in his eyes. Vivian smiled fondly. "My stomach always remembers a good cake," he said.

Claudia glanced between them, realizing just how much history had been building between her mother and Alex. How did she not know this?

"Well, tonight it will be stew and biscuits and maybe a cookie or two. Claudia and I made some sugar cookies for the bake sale last week, and I froze a few."

Alex's eyes lit up. "Sounds perfect."

But as they sat down for dinner, Claudia's unease returned. There was something deeper, unspoken, going on here. Later, when Alex was settling his bag into the guest room, Claudia finally asked, "What are you really doing here?"

"Can't I just miss you?" he asked, sitting on the edge of the bed and patting the spot next to him.

"Yes, I suppose so," she said, though she was still suspicious. "How have you been?" She sat beside him, and then she asked the question she didn't want to know the answer to. "Did you hear about the job?"

Alex's smile faded. "I did." His voice was softer now. "But it's just a job, Claudia. And I've been thinking. There's only one you. I don't want to lose you."

Her heart clenched as he spoke. "You'd give up your career for me?"

"In a heartbeat," he said, pulling her close. "When I thought I might lose you last week, I couldn't think of anything else."

Claudia closed her eyes, guilt rising in her chest. She'd been so tempted by the idea of Clint—of what could have been. But now, looking at Alex, she realized how close she'd come to losing everything she had.

"I never left," she whispered, though the words felt like a lie. She had considered it, more than once. Alex kissed her again, this time more urgently, as though he was trying to hold on to her, to everything they'd built.

"We should go downstairs before Mom comes looking for us," she said, breaking away. "But tonight... maybe we can talk about the job offer? Figure this out together?"

Alex nodded, though the unspoken tension between them lingered in the air. How could they bridge this gap

when the weight of their separate dreams threatened to
pull them apart?

CHAPTER 14

*A*fter dinner they went downtown to meet Rhys, who had gone ahead to find a good spot to watch the festive, decorated boats sail past the harbor.

"Alex! You came!" said Rhys, as Alex and Claudia approached.

"I said I would," Alex replied, clapping Rhys on the back. "Wouldn't miss it."

Claudia watched the pair, frowning in confusion. Since when were they this close? They seemed to be sharing inside jokes she had never heard before.

"I didn't even know these two talked," she murmured to her mother.

"Alex has always looked out for Rhys. They've known each other since Rhys was ten. He thinks of Alex as his uncle," her mother replied casually, as though it were common knowledge.

"I suppose that's true," Claudia admitted, though she hadn't fully realized how deep their connection went. Or how well Alex fit in with her family.

Her mother smiled knowingly. "Why don't you sit over there with Cam while Rhys plays? I'm going to track down the cocoa brigade."

"Sounds good," said Claudia, stepping off the path and onto the grass, where Rhys and Cam had spread out a couple of thick blankets. She sat down next to Cam, grateful it hadn't rained.

"I'm so glad the weather held up," Claudia said, smiling at Cam, who gave her a shy smile in return. "You must be freezing. You've been out here for a while. Thanks for getting the spot."

"I'm okay," said Cam. "Rhys made sure I had an extra blanket. He's done this before."

"He is pretty organized," said Claudia.

"Yeah," said Cam, glancing toward where Rhys was still talking to Alex. Her gaze lingered on him, the longing unmistakable. Claudia recognized that look all too well. It was the same way she used to look at Clint when she was that age.

As if on cue, Clint suddenly appeared in front of her.

"Can I talk to you a minute?" he asked.

Claudia stiffened, conscious of Alex and Rhys watching from a distance.

"Sure," she replied, her voice steady despite the tension she was feeling. "I'll be right back," she said to Cam, then she rose and walked a few steps away to speak to Clint.

"I talked to Yvette," Clint began. "She's open to trying again. She even mentioned visiting Vancouver. There are some good French immersion schools she's heard about, and she thinks she might be able to transfer jobs with her bank."

Claudia smiled. "That's wonderful news, Clint."

"I'm glad you were here to talk to," he said, his tone growing serious. "I've always had this… question mark when it came to us."

Claudia's breath caught in her throat. "What do you mean?"

"You know… the *what-ifs*," said Clint, his eyes searching hers.

She swallowed hard. "Yes. I know." Her voice was barely above a whisper. "I've wondered too. Why you left. What happened."

"I guess I needed closure," he admitted. "But I'm grateful I found it. I'm moving forward with Yvette, thanks to you."

Claudia nodded, feeling a strange mix of relief and finality.

Clint glanced over her shoulder, his expression shifting. "That guy over there—he's glaring at me like he wants to punch me. Who is he?"

Claudia followed his gaze to Alex's stony face. "That's Alex," she said. "He's here for the sailpast."

"The Alex you've been living with for the past six years?"

"Yes. My boyfriend," said Claudia.

"Well," Clint said with a small smile, "I should let you get back to him. I'll see you around."

"Sure. See you around," Claudia echoed, her heart pounding as Clint walked away.

Before she could collect her thoughts, Alex appeared beside her, his jaw tight. "Who was that guy?" His voice was calm, but the strain in his tone was unmistakable.

"Clint Jones," she answered, keeping her voice as steady as she could. "Tom's son."

"The same Clint Jones who left you to go to Australia?"

Claudia met his gaze, her heart sinking. "Yes."

"What's he doing here?"

"He's staying with his dad. Trying to figure out his marriage problems."

Alex studied her, his expression hard. "Claudia, I need you to tell me something, and I need you to be honest with me."

Her heart thudded in her chest. "Okay," she said cautiously.

"I wasn't completely honest with you when I said I just happened to come by to see Rhys play."

Claudia frowned. "Why did you come?"

Alex took a deep breath, his eyes locked on hers. "Because I found out Clint was in town. I heard he was single, and that you were spending time with him, and that… you might have feelings for him."

Her stomach dropped. "Who told you that?"

"Your nephew. He texted me, said you were upset and that an old boyfriend had shown up. So tell me, Claudia —what's going on? Is there something between you two?"

She opened her mouth, but no words came out. *Rhys?* she thought, stunned that her nephew would interfere like this. Then it hit her: her mother hadn't been surprised to see Alex either.

"My mother knew you were coming too, didn't she?" Claudia asked, her voice quieter now, a sharp edge to her words.

"Possibly," Alex admitted, his tone unreadable. "But that's not the point. You're avoiding my question."

Claudia's chest tightened as Alex's eyes bored into hers with a mix of anger and vulnerability. She knew he needed to hear the truth. "No," she said firmly. "There is nothing between us."

"You wouldn't lie to me?" he asked, his voice low, almost pleading.

Claudia exhaled slowly. "We had unfinished business. My mother was right—I hadn't completely let go of Clint. Not until this week. But now I have. He and I… We weren't meant to be together. He's meant to be with his wife, his family."

"And you?" Alex asked, his voice raw. "Where are you meant to be?"

"With you," she said softly. "If you'll still have me."

Alex searched her eyes, as if trying to see the truth behind her words. After a long moment, he nodded. "Come on," he said, his voice calmer now. "Cam has some friends here. How about you and I go for a walk? We need to talk."

He took her by the hand, guiding her away from the crowd. They walked together, up toward the hill, the sound of the band fading behind them as they sought

the privacy they needed to confront their truth
—together.

They walked in silence through the park until they
found an empty bench. Claudia's stomach churned with
nerves as she sat, bracing herself for what was coming.
Alex rarely got angry, but tonight felt different. She
knew her recent actions had pushed their relationship
into uncharted territory.

Alex exhaled slowly as he sat down beside her, his
fingers tapping lightly on his knee. "We need to make
some decisions, Claudia," Alex began, his voice steady
but filled with concern that made her pulse quicken. "I
don't want to go back home tomorrow still wondering
where we stand."

She nodded, her heart pounding. "Okay."

"We've been together for six years," he said, running a
hand through his hair, something he often did when he
was trying to find the right words. "And you know I
love you," he said, looking up into her eyes. His own
reflected uncertainty. "But these past few months, it
feels like we're being pulled in different directions."

Claudia's breath caught, she wanted to say something,
but waited for him to finish.

"I thought we wanted the same things, but maybe we haven't talked enough about what we do want—from this relationship, I mean."

"Alex."

"No." He held up his hand. "Let me finish. I've been thinking a lot about this. A few years ago, when we bought the condo, we talked about it being a first step."

"I remember," she said, grasping his hands. "Nothing's changed. I still love you, Alex."

"I love you too," he said softly, squeezing her hands with his, but there was a painful sincerity in his eyes. He released her. "But love isn't always enough, Claudia."

Her throat tightened. She wanted to scream, but she owed it to him to hear what he had to say. So she swallowed her panic. "I'm listening," she whispered.

"I've been giving things a lot of thought in the last year, especially since your father died." He paused as if again searching for the right words. "He was a good man. I admired how much he cared about his family, and how he was always there for your mother."

"He wasn't perfect," said Claudia, thinking about how her father had gone behind her back and warned off Clint all those years ago.

"No one's perfect," Alex continued, "but he had something I want. I want a family, Claudia. "I want that with you. I want a partner—my best friend—who wants the same."

"I want a family, too," she said quickly. "It's just that I also want a career."

"There's no reason you can't have both," Alex said gently. "You've been working at that agency for twelve years. You have the talent and skills to get a better job. I believe you can get one with even more impact. In fact, I think you owe it to yourself to reach higher."

"You really think so?" She searched his eyes and knew that he did. That he believed she could do better. The realization scared her—because what if he was wrong?

"Absolutely," he said, smiling. "I've always supported your career, Claudia. Just like you have always supported me."

Until recently. She blushed, thinking of how angry she'd been when she discovered the courses he had taken were preparing him for another career. And she lowered her eyes in shame when she realized she should have known. He had tried to tell her, and she hadn't listened. "I believe in you too, Alex," she said. "I'm sorry I haven't been supporting you as much this year."

"Thanks for saying that." He rubbed his hands on his pant legs. "But we have more to talk about."

"Yes," she whispered.

"Do you want to have children with me?"

"Yes," she said without hesitation. "But what if we can't? What if we try, and it doesn't happen?"

Alex's face tightened, and for a moment, she saw the flicker of fear in his eyes. He was always so composed, but this question shook him. "It would be hard," he admitted, "but if that's how things turn out, I'd accept it. I'd still want to be with you. If I had to face that, I wouldn't want to face it with anyone but you."

Her breath caught. The idea of not having kids was something she hadn't fully faced. And Alex—always so practical, so steady—was now looking more vulnerable than she'd ever seen him.

He straightened his posture. "Right. So the next to discuss is where we'll live."

Claudia's eyes narrowed. He was guiding the conversation like a negotiation now. "Don't lawyer me, Alex."

He turned sheepish, acknowledging her frustration. "Sorry. I've been thinking about this for a long time, but I haven't even asked why you want to stay in Vancouver."

"I like it there. I like our condo. I like being close to work."

"I like those things too," he agreed, "but if we're going to have a family, we'll need more space. We'll have to think about schools, safety, being close to our families."

She nodded, though the thought of moving felt like a shift in her entire life. "I guess my mom would love that," she said softly. "And your parents—they'd be great with a kid."

"That's why I've been thinking about moving to the island." His voice wavered, just for a moment. "And why I applied for that job."

Claudia's heart stopped. "You got it, didn't you?"

"Yes. I got an offer yesterday," he said. "I haven't accepted yet. I wanted to talk to you first."

She stared at him, disbelief creeping in. "Why didn't you say something yesterday?"

"I wanted to see how you felt about everything else before I decided. I wanted to talk to you in person. It's a great job, Claudia. I'd be working with seniors, helping protect them from financial abuse, neglect—things that really matter."

She nodded, biting her lip. "It's an important issue. At work, we've been looking into funding a program focused on elder abuse prevention."

"So you see why it's so important to me," he said, his voice softening. "It's not just about moving. It's about doing something meaningful."

Her stomach twisted. "You really want to take it, don't you?"

He hesitated, and the truth was clear on his face. "Yeah. I do. But not if it means I lose you. And not at the expense of your career."

The reality hit her like a wave. Moving, leaving her job, uprooting her life. But when she looked at him—really looked—she saw more than just the man she loved. She saw a future: a family, and a life with her best friend that they could build together.

"I've been thinking about it too," she said, her voice trembling. "My job isn't my career. It's a step. I know there are other organizations like it. But what we have is harder to replace. I don't want to lose us."

His eyes lit up with hope. "Claudia, I'd give it all up for you. If moving to the island means losing you, I'll stay. I'll turn down the job."

Tears welled up in her eyes. "Take the job, Alex. We can figure this out. It's an opportunity for both of us."

"Are you sure?"

"Yes. Let's do it. We'll sell the condo, start looking for a place on the island." Her heart raced with the decision, but for the first time in a long while, it was racing with excitement instead of dread. It felt right.

They would move forward together.

CHAPTER 15

*A*lex left in the morning, after breakfast and an early run, but not before learning about the mystery of the ornaments.

"You mean someone left you one yesterday and again today?" he asked, eyebrows raised in surprise.

"Yes! And we have no idea who it is," said Vivian. "I asked Tom about it, but he said it wasn't him. And it isn't Rhys or Claudia."

"So now you're on a mission to figure out who it is?" Alex laughed. "I have no doubt you'll solve it in no time."

But he was wrong.

The next day, there was no ornament on the tree. Disappointed, Vivian went on with her day. She started by putting out the trash for the first time since the day she'd tripped over Neville. When she was outside, Tom was walking past.

"Not taking Neville for a walk today?" she called.

He glanced up and down the street, then walked over to speak to her. "No Neville. I just took him back to Joe's. He and Helen got home last night."

"Well, that must be a relief," she teased.

"Actually, except for the few times he escaped, I enjoyed having him. I think I might like to get a dog. I certainly got out more. Had to walk Neville every day. And it's hard to be lonely with an animal in the house that follows you everywhere. You ever thought of having a pet?"

"I did, but Ned was allergic to them. It would have been too hard."

"Well, if you ever decide to get a dog, I'd be happy to take him for walks or watch him if you were in a pinch," he offered.

"If I do, you'll be the first to know." She laughed. "Say, how did it work out with your grandkids coming?"

"They'll be here on the twenty-third," he said. "I think it might work out, Viv. Clint is happy."

"Good. Claudia seems less stressed, too, since Alex visited this weekend. I'm glad. I like him. And Ned thought he was a good man."

They talked a little longer before saying goodbye, and Vivian had barely closed the garage door when her doorbell rang.

She ran to the front door. "Did you forget something?" she asked as she opened it. But instead of Tom, she found Helen on her doorstep. "Oh, hello, welcome back!"

"I know it's a little early to visit," Helen began, "but I'm stuck on central time, and I wanted to see how you were doing." She handed Vivian a small box wrapped in silver paper decorated with red Santa hats.

"You didn't need to bring me anything," said Vivian, taking the proffered gift.

"Oh, I didn't. I just found it on your porch. I don't see a card."

Vivian invited her friend in. "I wonder if this is the next one," she said. "Claudia," she called out, "I think the third one has arrived."

Claudia came out of her room to say hello to Helen and watch as her mother opened the box.

"What is this all about?" asked Helen.

"Mom has received two ornaments. We think someone is giving her gifts like Dad used to do."

"This one is beautiful," said Vivian, after ripping off the paper and opening the box. Nestled in some red tissue was an ornament made of wood: a carved hen intricately painted, with the number three hanging below. "The first two were made of tin and this one is wood, but they all have the same kind of numbers on them."

"It looks a little like one I saw last year at the Community Tree Festival," said Helen. "I was sorry to miss it this year, and Joe was devastated. He always decorates a tree."

"Maybe that's where they were purchased," said Claudia. "Or they might be available in town somewhere. Though I haven't seen any like them."

"I'll look around when I'm in town today," said Helen. "Which is why I stopped by. We had plans to go for lunch, but I was wondering if we could also do some shopping? Make a day of it?"

"I'd love to. Claudia is working all day anyway."

"Needs must," said Claudia with a false frown. "Have fun."

They headed downtown and poked around in the stores for a couple of hours before going to Whisking Love, their favorite bistro. After a leisurely lunch, Helen asked, "Do you want to come with me while I run some more errands, or should I drop you home?"

Vivian shook her head. "I don't have anything to do at home. Rhys is at school taking an exam, and it's just me and the TV. I'd rather be out with you."

They spent the afternoon shopping, and eventually wandered into the fabric store, where Gemma greeted them warmly.

"Hi, Vivian," Gemma said, turning to her. "Did Claudia talk to you about the workshops?"

"No, unless I don't remember," Vivian replied. "My

memory is terrible these days. The internet tells me it's down to my grief."

Gemma's face softened. "I'm so sorry about Ned. You must miss him terribly."

"I do," Vivian said with a wistful smile. "But I'm trying to enjoy the season. He would have wanted that."

Gemma nodded. "I was wondering if you'd consider teaching a beginners' class on Thursdays. I'm having trouble finding someone to help."

"Tell me more," Vivian said, intrigued.

"The morning class is for a few women who need help learning to knit," Gemma explained. "The afternoon class is for kids, mostly twelve and up, who are interested in making crocheted animals like the ones you're teaching Claudia to make."

Vivian thought for a moment. "I'd be delighted."

Gemma brightened. "I'll pay you, of course. Maybe you can come down the first Tuesday after New Year's, and we'll go over the details."

"That sounds like fun," Vivian agreed, warming to the idea.

Gemma looked relieved. "Now all I need is help in the store for Tuesdays and Wednesdays. I could really use an extra hand."

"Would you consider me for that too?" Vivian asked, surprising herself.

Gemma blinked. "In the fabric department? You've been sewing for years—of course!"

Vivian smiled. "I'd love to help."

Gemma's excitement was palpable. "Thank you so much, Vivian. I'm looking forward to working with you. I'll send you the details by email. I'm pretty sure I still have your address."

As they left the store, Vivian turned to Helen. "Well, what do you think of that? I'm about to be gainfully employed again after ten years of retirement!"

Helen hugged her. "It's the beginning of a whole new adventure. I'm so proud of you for putting yourself out there again. I've missed the old Vivian."

Vivian chuckled. "I've missed me too. And I have you to thank for it."

"Me?" Helen raised an eyebrow.

"You left Neville with Tom, and that little rascal knocked me on my butt," Vivian said with a laugh. "I needed it."

Helen shook her head, amused. "I'm sure you didn't need the bumps and bruises, but I admire your ability to find the silver lining. Between you and me, I love Neville, but I also love when he goes home in January."

"It must be nice to have the company, though. Tom certainly enjoyed having him."

"Would you like a dog?" Helen asked.

"I've been thinking about it—maybe a rescue. One that's more sedate than Neville."

"And one not bent on being the Houdini of the dog world," Helen added with a laugh. "He got out of the yard again this morning, chasing after the cat. Poor Joe had to fix the fence the moment he got back from vacation. He wasn't thrilled, especially with three custom orders to fill this week."

"Yes, if I get a dog, it will be more sedate," Vivian mused. "Definitely."

By Tuesday, another ornament had appeared on the tree —four calling birds—yet still no sign of who was behind the gifts. Claudia's mind spun with possibilities. Maybe it was one of the neighbors, like Jack or Sylvia, who owned Angel. She'd ask them when they came to her open house on Boxing Day. Claudia had convinced her to keep the tradition alive this year, since she and Rhys would be around to help.

Wednesday, day five, was a whirlwind. Vivian helped Rhys make dinner—or, more accurately, she watched as he expertly prepared a roast beef with all the fixings. When Karen and Adrian arrived home from Mexico, Vivian laughed out loud at their astonished faces.

"What happened?" Adrian asked, wide-eyed. "See, Karen? Necessity is the mother of invention after all. Leave a kid to cook his own food, and he'll learn to do it."

CHAPTER 16

When Karen walked into her mother's house, she felt as though she'd walked into the twilight zone. When she had left, her mother had been noncommunicative bordering on surly. It had made her want to visit less and less often, until she had let the visits slip, making excuses not to come as often. She had been fully prepared to have Claudia on her side by the time she got back, and together they would help their mother pick out a care facility and move her in within six months.

Now it was as though they had gone back in time. This was her mother of years past, and she wasn't sure what to make of it.

After dinner, she cornered her sister in the kitchen under the guise of helping with the dishes.

"What happened?"

"What do you mean?" asked Claudia, scraping the contents of a dish into the compost bin.

"Mom. What happened? When I left, she was hardly communicating. Now she's out there chatting up a storm."

Claudia put the dish into the dishwasher and turned toward Karen. "When I arrived, Mom was in hospital," she said, her voice tinged with anger.

"What are you talking about?"

"You told me to come that evening, but on the way, Rhys called me. He was panicked, and between him and Clint, they phoned the ambulance. I went straight there."

"Did she fall again?" Karen asked, horrified and wracked with guilt.

"No. She decided that, because it hurt too much to get up and go to the bathroom, she just wouldn't drink anything. It was dehydration."

Karen pushed her hands through her hair in frustration. "Why didn't you tell me?"

Claudia just looked at her, her eyebrow lifted. "Why do you think?"

"Because she told you not to," said Karen, knowing exactly how that conversation would have gone. "How long was she in there?"

"Just two nights. They kept her an extra day to make sure she had enough fluids."

"But then what did you do? She seems like a different person now."

"Tom, Clint, Rhys, and I decided to make a project out of it. The doctor said she was depressed—she still needs to see her doctor about that so she doesn't have a relapse—and suggested we get her out, spend time with her, get her involved in the community again."

"And she agreed?"

"I think she didn't want to disappoint Rhys. He has been so good with her, and she's been teaching him how to cook. Although judging by the dinner tonight, the kid's already got some serious skills."

"He did a good job, didn't he?" said Karen. "I'm glad he's been spending time with Mom. She seems so much better."

"And she got herself a job yesterday, teaching knitting at Gemma's shop."

"Really," Karen said, relieved. "I was thinking we would need to find her a home."

"I think she's got a lot of good years in her yet. She was even talking to Tom about getting a dog."

"A dog? I didn't think she even liked dogs. Especially since Neville knocked her down."

"She says it's the best bad thing that ever happened to her," said Claudia.

"Thank you," said Karen. "I'm sorry that I dragged you here against your will, but I am so glad you came. You and Rhys did more for Mom in two weeks than I have been able to do in months. Especially with the ornaments. You have her flummoxed."

"That's not me," said Claudia.

"Then who?"

"Not sure, but I'm betting on Santa Claus."

CHAPTER 17

Thursday and Friday brought new surprises: five golden rings, carefully hung on the tree, and a goose nestled in a small basket on the doorstep. There was still no return address or hint of who was giving these wonderful gifts.

Tom had denied having any part in it, and Helen hadn't even been around when the ornaments started appearing, so Vivian was at a loss to know who to thank.

On Friday night, Karen's eldest, Jessie, came to visit, newly back from university. She swooped to give Claudia and Vivian huge hugs. "I missed you so much," she said to her grandmother.

Vivian laughed. "I think you missed the chocolate chip cookies more."

Jessie laughed, reaching for a cookie and dipping it into her hot cocoa. "Okay, maybe a little." She spent the next hour telling her grandmother all about school, while Claudia retreated to finish up work before Alex arrived the next morning. As much as she had enjoyed the past week, she missed him.

The following morning, they spied a swan hanging from the tree, dusted with snow that had begun to fall the night before. Worried about the weather, Claudia phoned to confirm Alex was still coming. But he was already on his way.

"I can't remember the last time we had this much snow!" Claudia huffed later, leaning on her shovel in her mother's driveway, now clear of snow. "I hope Alex can make it."

"I'm sure he'll be along soon," said Vivian, as she spread salt over the asphalt. "He's a good driver, and the snow has nearly stopped." She waved her hand up at the sky.

. . .

*S*uddenly, Helen came scurrying along the sidewalk. "Neville!" she called out. "Have you seen Neville?"

Claudia set the shovel against the house. "No, but I'll help you find him."

"Wait for me!" Vivian hurried to join them.

Tom joined the search as they passed by his house. "Maybe he's by the school," he suggested. "That's his favorite spot."

Sure enough, they spotted Neville gleefully chasing a group of children who were sledding down the hill. Claudia pointed him out, laughing at the sight. "How are we going to get him to come here?"

Vivian's eyes twinkled mischievously. "The old-fashioned way." She approached a group of kids with a toboggan. "I need to rescue my dog," she explained, commandeering the sled.

Claudia's jaw dropped. "You're not really going to—"

"Of course I am," Vivian said with a grin, climbing onto the sled. "Helen, bring the leash!"

Helen laughed and climbed onto the back of the toboggan, grabbing Vivian around the waist.

"Ready?" asked Tom. Before Claudia could protest, Tom gave them a push, and they sailed down the hill. Claudia's heart pounded in her chest as they flew toward Neville.

"What if they crash?" she fretted.

Tom chuckled. "What if they don't? Look at them—they're having a blast."

The kids who owned the taboggan ran down the hill after them, and Claudia followed, agog at her mother, who expertly steered the toboggan until she stopped gracefully next to Neville, who wagged his tail in excitement.

Helen scooped him up, while Vivian returned the toboggan with a smile.

"I can't believe you did that!" said Claudia, finally catching up with them.

"You got us into trouble again, Neville," Vivian said, laughing so hard that Claudia couldn't help but join in.

Later that afternoon, as they gathered for coffee, Claudia listened to her mother, Helen, and Tom as they reminisced about their younger days. She could hardly believe the woman laughing by the fire was the same one she had worried over in the hospital just a week before.

By the time the milkmaid, dancing lady, leaping lord, and piper joined the decorations on the tree, Vivian was looking healthier than ever. But the identity of the ornament-giver remained a mystery.

As Christmas Eve fell, Claudia snuggled up with Alex. "I still can't figure out who's been leaving the ornaments," she said, her eyes closing as she drifted to sleep.

"Maybe we'll find out tomorrow," he whispered, pulling her close.

On Christmas morning, Claudia woke to find Alex watching her, his head propped on his hand.

"Merry Christmas, sleepyhead," he said with a grin.

"Merry Christmas," she replied, smiling. "Is Mom already up?"

"About an hour ago. She's baking scones for breakfast. Your sister and her family should be here soon."

Claudia groaned. "I should help her."

Alex gently stopped her. "Not so fast. I have a present for you first."

"We said no gifts this year," she reminded him.

"We agreed on experiences, remember?" he teased. "But I thought I'd make an exception."

Curious, Claudia took the small box he handed her. It was wrapped in paper she had seen before.

Her eyes widened. "It was you!"

Alex feigned innocence. "What was me?"

"You've been leaving the presents for Mom!"

"Now how could I have done that?" he asked, looking abashed.

"I don't know, but you were definitely involved. Don't lie to me, Alex."

He laughed, holding up his hands. "Okay, yes. But I had help. Helen, Joe, and Tom pitched in."

Claudia's heart warmed. "It's brought her so much joy."

"We did it for your dad," Alex said softly. "He planned it all before he passed."

Her breath caught. "How?"

"I got a letter from his lawyer, along with the ornaments. He wanted to make sure this Christmas was special."

Tears welled in Claudia's eyes. "And you kept it a secret this whole time?"

"I had to," Alex grinned. "It wouldn't have been the same if you'd known."

She threw her arms around him. "Thank you."

As they embraced, Alex gestured to the little box still in her hand. "Aren't you going to open it?"

Claudia's heart pounded as she unwrapped it, revealing… nothing. She looked up at Alex in confusion, but he was now on one knee.

"I know we always said we don't need a piece of paper between us, but over this past year, I've realized I want something more. I want forever with you. So, Claudia, will you marry me?"

Claudia's heart swelled with joy. "Yes," she whispered, tears in her eyes. "Yes, yes, yes!"

CHAPTER 18

*V*ivian sat in Ned's old recliner, the little drummer boy figurine catching the morning light on the table beside her. Tears streamed down her face as she held a letter in her trembling hands.

"Oh, Ned... I miss you so much," she whispered, her voice barely audible.

Claudia rushed into the room, excitement lighting up her face. "Mom! Guess what!" She stopped abruptly when she saw her mother's tear-streaked face. "Mom, are you okay?"

Vivian looked up, handing Claudia the letter that had

come with the gift. Claudia took it, her eyes scanning the shaky handwriting.

My love,

I hope this Christmas is as wonderful as our last one together. I can almost taste the turkey and imagine our family gathered around the table, sharing in the delightful feast you have no doubt provided.

I asked Alex to help me give you one last gift—one last "Twelve Days"—to remind you how deeply I love you and how much you mean to me. You are my light, my heart, the love of my life.

Leaving you before we were ready has been the hardest thing I ever had to do, but I hope you carry with you the knowledge that you were cherished, always. Find reasons to keep giving to others the boundless love and care you always provide.

And seek companionship—love—in your life until we meet again.

Thank you for all the beautiful moments you gave me.

Love always,

Ned

Claudia's throat tightened as she handed the letter back. "Oh, Mom… he loved you so much."

"Yes," Vivian whispered. "And even now, after he's gone, he found a way to make this Christmas special."

The doorbell rang, pulling them from their reverie.

"That must be your sister," Vivian said, dabbing her eyes.

But when Claudia opened the door, it wasn't her sister. Helen stood there, her little Westie Neville sitting at her feet in a tiny Santa hat.

"Merry Christmas!" Helen exclaimed. "We were out on our walk and wanted to stop by. Neville has a gift for you."

The little dog barked excitedly, and Helen handed a small box to Vivian.

"What have you brought me?" Vivian asked, her voice soft but curious.

"Joe felt awful about your fall, so he wanted to make you something special," Helen explained.

Vivian carefully opened the box. Inside was a delicate glass ornament, one of Joe's handmade creations. It depicted a little white Westie and a black cat sitting together by a Christmas tree, their tiny figures aglow with holiday cheer.

Vivian's eyes filled with tears again, but this time they were happy ones.

"I'll treasure this always," she said softly, holding the ornament up to show Claudia. "It's a reminder of what a gift Neville gave me this year. He reminded me that even though Ned is gone… there is still love."

She paused, her gaze far away but peaceful.

"Because that's what life is all about, isn't it?" Vivian murmured, her voice steady and sure. "Love."

EPILOGUE

*R*hys and Adrian were standing in front of a pile of yellow-gold leaves from the old pear tree when Alex and Claudia pulled their car into the driveway on the second Sunday of October.

"You're here early," said Adrian, holding out a yard bag while Rhys put the leaves inside.

"Grandma is in the kitchen," said Rhys, frowning in concentration as he added more leaves to the bag.

"I thought you'd be helping, what with all your newfound culinary skills," said Claudia, chuckling as she walked over to give her nephew a hug and then turning to hug Adrian.

"I'm just taking a break," said Rhys. "I made the stuffing, and I'm going to make Grandma's recipe for baked brussels sprouts, but Mom wanted to learn how to make the dessert."

"Do you need a hand with this?" asked Alex, shaking Adrian's hand.

"No. We're almost done. You go ahead."

Alex picked up their overnight bag and climbed the front steps after Claudia, who knocked and then opened the door. "Mom?" she called.

"Oh, you're here," said Vivian, coming out to the living room and wiping her hands on her apron. "How was your honeymoon trip?"

Claudia turned to look up at Alex and smiled. "Paris was fantastic, wasn't it?"

He set their bag down. "We had a great time. Just the thing to do when you're waiting for your house to be updated."

"So the contractors finished the renos? And your move went well?"

"We still have some things to unpack, but everything went in on Thursday," said Claudia. "We'd like to have you and Karen and family down to visit soon. Maybe the long weekend in November?"

"I can't wait," said Karen, coming out of the kitchen to meet them. "The pictures you sent were beautiful."

"And wait until you see the neighbourhood," said Claudia, taking off her coat and hanging it in the closet. "It's perfect. And it's close for Alex to go to work."

"How is *your* job hunt going?" asked Vivian, leading them into the living room and urging them to have a seat.

"Well, it's coming along, but meanwhile I'm able to keep my job. After I showed them I could work remotely when I was here last year, they agreed I could keep going for at least another six months. I just have to travel back for meetings a few times a month."

"Excellent news," said Vivian. "Your father would be so happy for you."

"Yes, I do believe he would," said Claudia. She noticed that, for the first time since losing him, she could think of her father without having to hold back tears.

"Listen," said Alex. "We have—"

"What is that noise?" asked Claudia, cutting him off before he could say more and giving him a warning look.

He shrugged and got up to look out the window, smiling when he saw what was happening outside. "Let's give them a hand, shall we?" He shoved his feet into his shoes and opened the door. Claudia followed, chuckling at the sight in front of her.

Vivian looked out the window and laughed. "Meanwhile, I'll make us all some hot chocolate."

As Claudia stepped outside, Rhys yelled, "Neville!" She laughed out loud at the little Westie, who was jumping in the leaves, barking, and moving just out of reach of her nephew. Adrian was leaning on the rake, laughing, and Helen, leash in hand, was now rushing into the yard.

"I'm sorry," said Helen, looking apologetic. "I just turned away for a second."

Alex helped Rhys corner the little dog, then picked him up. Neville yapped happily, licking Alex's face as if to say, *Hey, I missed you guys!*

Helen snapped the leash onto his collar, and Alex set the dog down.

"Since we're all here," said Alex, bending down to pat Neville, "I wanted to ask if you think we should do another round of Vivian's twelve days of Christmas."

"She won't be expecting it," said Adrian. "It's a great idea."

"I'll send you all an email," said Alex, taking the rake from Adrian. "Let me help Rhys out here. Adrian, maybe you can ask Tom if he wants to help." He nodded toward Tom, who was approaching from next door. Neville barked in recognition and pulled Helen toward his old friend.

"Hello, young fella," said Tom, bending down to pat the dog.

Adrian released the rake, looking grateful for the break, and Claudia silently thanked Alex. He always seemed to know just when someone needed something, a gift she appreciated more and more as the years passed.

Rhys and Alex quickly finished up the leaves while Claudia chatted a few minutes with Helen and then followed them all into the house.

.   .   .

wo hours later, as they sat around the table at the end of their Thanksgiving meal, they took turns sharing what they were thankful for this year.

"I'm thankful that I passed my calculus final," said Rhys. "And that we finally got all those leaves raked up."

His father laughed. "I'm also glad about the leaves, but I'm thankful for my improved health and for the health of my family."

Karen followed him by saying, "I'm thankful that Mom is so much more active than she was last year."

"Hear, hear," said Alex. "I'm thankful for officially becoming part of this family," he said. "And for this fantastic Battenberg cake. Thanks, Vivian."

"I think you can stop calling me Vivian now, Alex. Call me Mom."

"That reminds me," said Alex, looking at Claudia and raising his eyebrows in question.

She smiled. "Go ahead, then."

He grinned and looked around the table. "I'm thankful for something else, too. In the spring, Claudia will get a new name. She will also be called Mom."

"What?" said Vivian "This is fantastic news! Congratulations. How do you feel, my dear?"

"Excited," said Claudia. "Nervous. Tired. I guess I'm feeling lots of things. But"—she reached over and took Alex's hand—"whatever comes next, I'm thankful I have my best friend along the journey with me."

"Yes." Alex bent to kiss her on the cheek. "Whatever comes next, we will face it together."

"What about you, Grandma?" asked Rhys. "What are you thankful for?"

"I am grateful I have all of you to make my life so rich and worthwhile," said Vivian. "And I am grateful that I tripped over Neville."

"To Neville," said Adrian, lifting his water glass in a toast. "May he never change."

"Hear, hear!" They all raised their glasses, and dissolved into laughter.

uthor's Note:

Dear Reader,

I hope you enjoyed A Partridge in Sunshine Bay. If you're looking for more heartwarming tales check out the other books in the Sunshine Bay and Shops at Sunshine Bay series to see what's happening with the town's other residents!

To be the first to know about what is coming next stop by my website and sign up for my newsletter at www.-JeanineLauren.com.

And if you loved the festive charm of Vivian's journey, please consider leaving a review. Reviews are an incredible way to support indie authors like me, so I can continue bringing you more stories from Sunshine Bay.

Until next time, happy reading!

Jeanine

ABOUT THE AUTHOR

Jeanine Lauren is a USA Today bestselling author who crafts heartwarming women's fiction and sweet romance, celebrating friendship, love, community, and second chances.

After a lifetime of writing for school, day jobs, and those endless 'to-do' lists we all ignore, Jeanine finally turned her passion into publishing in 2019 with Love's Fresh Start, the first book in her Sunshine Bay series. Now, she's racing to make up for lost time, writing as fast as she can to bring more of Sunshine Bay to life.

Want to know when the next book is out? Join her mailing list for updates!

Jeanine calls the lower mainland of British Columbia home, just a stone's throw from the fictional town of Sunshine Bay where her characters' stories unfold.

ALSO BY JEANINE LAUREN

Sunshine Bay

Love's Fresh Start

Come Home To Love

Angel and the Neville Next Door

The Shops at Sunshine Bay

The Bookworm and The Cat's Meow

Making Sweet Music

Christmas Trees and Mistletoe

Shopping for Love in Cataluma

Something of Note: A Sweet Second Chance Romance

Lost Loves, Found

Repositioning: Lost Love, Found

Novelettes

Snowed in With You

Kayaks and Kisses

Made in the USA
Las Vegas, NV
11 November 2024

11622687R00132